MY FAKE BOYFRIEND IS BETTER THAN YOURS

MY FAKE BOYFRIEND IS BETTER THAN YOURS

Kristina Springer

SCHOLASTIC INC.
New York Toronto London Auckland
Sydney Mexico City New Delhi Hong Kong

ISBN 978-0-545-33605-5

Copyright © 2010 by Kristina Springer. All rights reserved.
Published by Scholastic Inc., 557 Broadway, New York, NY
10012, by arrangement with Farrar, Straus and Giroux, Inc.
SCHOLASTIC and associated logos are trademarks and/or
registered trademarks of Scholastic Inc.

12 11 10 9 8 7 6 5 4 3 2 1   11 12 13 14 15 16/0

Printed in the U.S.A.   40

First Scholastic printing, January 2011

Designed by Natalie Zanecchia

TO MOM,
FOR ALWAYS BEING
THERE FOR ME,
THROUGH BFFS
AND BOYFRIENDS

MY FAKE BOYFRIEND IS BETTER THAN YOURS

1

We're outta here in ten, Tor!" Mom screams from the bathroom down the hallway.

I look at the two outfits carefully laid out on my bed for the fiftieth time this morning. I can't decide what to wear. I have the still-new turquoise spaghetti strap sundress that looks really cute on me but that I never managed to wear all summer. I just didn't have anywhere to wear it. Or I have my new "Go Green" T-shirt and recycled jeans. The dress says I had a great summer and don't want it to end. But the eco-friendly outfit makes a statement and shows I'm environmentally aware. Of course, the dress might make people think I'm trying too hard. Which I obviously am. Then again, so might the green outfit. Argh! This is hard. I've never had to pick out the all-important first day of school outfit on my own before. Sienna and I always had our outfits down weeks beforehand.

"You're still not dressed?" Mom asks, appearing in my doorway. She's already in a silk top and a skirt, ready for work.

"I will be. Just a sec."

"Seriously, Tori, you've got five minutes and then you're busing it."

"Okay, okay," I say, shutting the door. I grab the green outfit and change quickly. The sundress would have been a lie anyway. The summer totally blew. And it's all Sienna's fault.

I check my reflection in the mirror and give my mostly straight brown hair one final brush. I can't help, for the thousandth time this summer, thinking about Sienna. Why hasn't she called me? Or e-mailed? Texted? Anything? We've been best friends since kindergarten and it was bad enough that I had to endure the entire summer without her while she and her family were in Florida. Torturous, really. But what is with the silent treatment these last six weeks? She didn't have a single minute to send one lousy postcard? I know that she's rich and all now, but that's even more reason for her to send me a postcard. Make that a hundred postcards.

Sea started out the summer e-mailing me every day—long e-mails detailing everything from the starfish she saw swept up on the beach to the seagull that pooped on the front window of their rental car. Then the e-mails started tapering off, getting shorter and shorter and farther in between. I kept writing, of course, even though she never answered any of my questions or commented on what was going on in my life. The last e-mail I got was six weeks ago and it only said, "I'm getting ready to go out for dinner." That's it. Nothing more. If I was more paranoid I'd think some bad guys kidnapped her entire family at an all-you-can-eat seafood buffet and she's locked in a dingy basement somewhere without wireless access. I'm not paranoid though, so the only other thing that could have happened is Sea is ignoring me. But why?

"I'll be in the car," Mom yells, and I hear the front door slam shut.

"I'm coming," I holler back, but of course she can't hear me. I slip my backpack over my shoulders and race for the door, only stopping briefly to grab a strawberry fruit bar from the pantry.

Mom is tapping her fingers impatiently on the steering wheel when I climb in. "Sorry, Mom," I say. The car smells overwhelmingly peachy from the candle-shaped air freshener she has hanging from the rearview mirror.

Mom takes a deep breath through her nose. "No, I'm sorry, sweets. It's just I have this really important meeting in fifteen minutes and I can't be late. But it's your first day. Are you excited? Need money?" She plucks a ten from her purse and hands it to me while reversing out of the driveway and into traffic. Mom's a multitasking goddess.

"Thanks." I take the money and tuck it into the front pocket of my backpack. I stare out the window, watching the passing oak trees and street signs with the names of various presidents. We're both silent for a few blocks.

"Nervous?" Mom asks. She's steering with her knees. I hate when she does this. Nine and three, *nine and three*, I always want to say. I'm only twelve and even *I* know you're supposed to keep your hands at nine and three on the steering wheel. Mom pulls a bottle of hand lotion out of the center console, squirts some into her palm, and rubs her hands together. More peach. I don't like peaches.

I shrug.

"It'll be great, honey. Promise." She returns one hand to the steering wheel and dives back into her purse with the other, searching for something.

"Uh-huh," I reply. She says the same thing every year on the first day of school and it's never reached "great" yet. But it's usually been tolerable since Sienna and I have always faced school together. But I don't know about this year. Are we even friends anymore? Did I do something? Does she hate me now? If she does, she could've at least let me know. It's completely unfair to just hate a person and not tell her.

Last year on the first day of school, Sea came to my house at 6:30 in the morning in her pj's, toting her clothes in a duffel bag. Our moms thought we were being silly, but we were determined to get dressed for school together. We both wore jeans but I wore a pretty mint green peasant top and Sea wore a white, fitted tuxedo shirt, complete with the old-fashioned ruffles down the middle. We looked *really* good.

It was a last-minute decision to do our nails in the vampy black polish I'd picked up while shopping with Mom for back-to-school supplies. Sea said it was very *Teen Vogue* and would be the perfect first-day accent.

And it was. For like a minute. But then I got a big glob of vampy black on the right shoulder of my new shirt in an unfortunate hand-waving/nail-blowing incident. Of course Mom chose that precise moment to yell that we had to get in the car *right now*. I looked at Sea, completely freaked. This was the perfect shirt. I didn't have a backup outfit. Sienna didn't panic though. She searched around my desk and then plunged a dry hand into my seashell jewelry box, filled with miscellaneous odds and ends. She pulled out my "Hug a Tree" button and pinned it over the black spot.

"Perfect," she said. But I wasn't so sure. I didn't want to look like a big dork with a button on the shoulder of my shirt on the first day of school. My face must have showed this because then Sea dove into my jewelry box again and pulled out a "Save the Whales" button and pinned it on her shirt in the exact same spot. No one said anything to us about our buttons and maybe we both looked dorky but it didn't matter. I remember I felt a million times better because of Sea that day.

Mom pulls into the Norton Junior High School parking lot and I fidget in my seat. I don't want to get out of the car and start the new school year. See the same students again. The same teachers. I just want to go back home where it's safe and hide in my room with a stack of books. It's pretty much what I did all summer and I'm not quite finished yet.

We stop near the main doors and Mom looks at me with a big smile. "Have a great day, hon. And call me as soon as you get home after school, okay? Remember, no Internet while I'm not home."

I nod but don't move.

"C'mon, Tor. It'll be fine," she assures me. "Go find Sienna."

If Sienna is even here, I think. Maybe her dad took all that new money he made in the stock market last spring and decided to buy them a permanent home in the

Keys rather than just summer there. Maybe he bought her a dozen tutors to sit with her poolside and teach her everything. Maybe he sprang to have a superchip containing every bit of information she'd need to know up through high school implanted in her brain so she doesn't even have to go to school anymore. Now *that* would be cool.

"Seriously, Tor. I have five minutes to make my meeting." Mom hands me my backpack and gives my shoulder a nudge.

"Okay, okay." I sigh and get out of the car. I step up onto the sidewalk and watch my mom pull away from the curb, waving. But I don't wave back. She isn't looking at me anyway.

I remember the day Sienna found out she was loaded like it was yesterday. We were sitting at her kitchen table, cutting pictures of Zane Stewart, the hottie lead singer of the Green Beans, out of magazines to make a collage. Her mom was scrubbing at a scraped-up baker's rack and mumbling curse words about the quality of fiberboard furniture these days. Her dad, whom I've only ever seen on weekends because of his long work hours during the week, came swooping in with a fancy-looking bottle of champagne. He yelled a bunch of stuff about being rich, swung his wife around in a circle, and picked up Sea like she was still five years old.

Everybody was really happy. And I was happy for them too, of course. Sea said nothing would really change. They wouldn't move to a fancy house and she wouldn't transfer to a fancy school. And I'm not saying she lied or anything, but maybe she just didn't know that things would change.

I smooth my T-shirt over my hips and cross my arms over my chest. I look around the courtyard, which is swarming with perky, excited students. No one wants to go into school yet. Everyone's too busy checking out each other's new cell phones and iPods. Both of which are banned inside school. I glance from group to group—the mini fashionistas, the mathletes, the band kids—trying to decide where to go stand until first bell, when my eyes fall on a group of girls huddled around someone. Probably an eighth grader showing off her new designer purse. I'm about to turn away and check the side of the school building when I hear her laugh. Sienna.

My heart beats faster and I'm filled with relief. Thank God she's here. I was really starting to think I'd be doing seventh grade without her. I run for the group of girls. "Sea!" I yell, nudging past a few of them.

Long, beautifully highlighted, low-lighted, flat-ironed hair swooshes in front of me as she turns and we come face-to-face.

I scrunch up my face and peer into her eyes. "Si-enna?" I ask.

She laughs. "Tori! Oh, Tori, I missed you." She throws her tanned arms around my neck and squeezes hard. I peer down at her right shoulder near my cheek. How is she tan? In the seven years I've known Sienna she's never done more than burn in the sun. Is it makeup or something? I rub my fingers on her shoulder and then look at them. Nope. Nothing came off. And that hair?

"Your hair . . ." I begin, pulling back from her embrace.

She laughs again. "You like?" She shakes her head, and her long blond hair glistens in the sun.

"Yeah. I love. But it was short, brown, and curly in May. How'd you do this?" *And why didn't you mention it in one of your e-mails?*

She leans close and whispers in my ear, "Extensions."

"Oh," I say, but still don't quite understand. The only extension I've ever had was when I needed extra time on a homework assignment. But her hair looks so real. I reach out to touch it and she laughs and moves away before I do.

"So how was your summer?" she asks.

A wave of emotions washes over me. Part anger at Sea

for dropping off the face of the earth in July, and part relief that she's actually here. She looks at me, waiting for an answer. "Well, uh . . . great," I say, suddenly very self-conscious. There are all these girls still standing around us, listening to every word we say. We're not even friends with most of these girls. Heck, I don't think we've ever even talked to half of them before. They were always "too good" to associate with us. Not that we needed them or anything; Sea and I always had each other.

I want to ask what happened—why she stopped writing me. But I don't want to put her on the defensive by attacking her the first minute I talk to her. "And you?" I ask, bracing myself for the What I Did on My Summer Vacation essay to end all essays.

Sienna giggles. "Oh my god, Tori, it was *so* fabulous. I have to tell you all about it."

Nice. Now she wants to tell me about it. I nod but I'm starting to get weirded out. The other girls still haven't left and in fact are staring at Sienna with big eyes and bigger smiles. Like she's a celebrity or something. And granted, she does look nice. She's got on a super cute navy blue baby-doll dress and she's tan everywhere —down to her perfectly pedicured toes. And dang, she's got on three-inch wedge sandals. For school. My mom still won't let me wear one-inch heels to weddings.

"To start with, the house we stayed in had eighteen bedrooms. Eighteen! I had three to myself alone. And it was right on the beach. I could open my patio doors and walk down to the water, day or night." Hmm. I already know all of this. Sienna described the house in full detail—down to the bidet with the brass angel knob in her personal bathroom—in her very first vacation e-mail. I'm starting to feel like I'm in a play, only I wasn't provided with a script. She closes her eyes and sniffs the air. I take a quick sniff too. What is she smelling? Did the wind shift and we're getting the sewage plant breeze again? She opens her eyes and looks at me. "Sometimes I can almost still smell the ocean air," she adds.

Oh. Ocean air. Right. "Wow. Well, it sounds amazing," I say, hoping my intense jealousy won't leak out all over the place and make a mess.

Sienna nods. "Daddy rented a yacht for the entire summer too and he even let me drive it a couple of times. When we were far from shore, of course."

"Of course," I agree. Like I know. My dad still won't let me drive the grocery cart when we're shopping.

"And then—" she starts, but she's interrupted by Justin Timberlake. One of his songs, anyway. "Oh, hold on." She slips one hand into a large leather purse, pulls out a pink-sleeved iPhone, and holds it to her ear.

"Hello?" she says, and then instantly dissolves into giggles. "Oh, hi, Antonio."

Antonio? That's a boy's name, right? So, there's a boy named Antonio calling her.

Who is this girl and what did she do with my best friend?

2

I involuntarily take a step back. Involuntarily because the group of girls has edged in closer to Sienna and bumped me from the circle.

I survey the other students outside. The air is buzzing with first-day excitement. There are always so many possibilities at the start of each school year. Of course, each year usually ends up much like the previous one, and we fool ourselves into thinking the new one will be better. But not this year. This year is *definitely* different.

Sienna rejoins me outside the circle. "Sorry about that. Antonio wanted to see how school was going so far." She drops her phone back into her purse.

"Who?" I ask.

Her face lights up and she puts one hand on my forearm. "Antonio," she whispers. "I'm in love!" she says louder, obviously not for my benefit. My hearing is just fine.

The going-nowhere group of girls let out a chorus of *aww*s. Sienna nods, like she's confirming their *aww*s or something. "He's amazing. He's tall and handsome and so sweet and I met him in the Keys this summer."

"So, you have a boyfriend now?" I notice the circle of girls has re-formed around the two of us. Looks like I'm back onstage.

Sienna smiles. "Well, yeah . . ."

The girls oooh and giggle.

Okay. Really? This is beginning to feel a little too *High School Musical.* I halfway expect these girls to start synchronized dancing and singing in a circle around Sienna while she dishes about her new dude. And how does she even have a new dude? I mean, this *is* Sienna. Last year she would have turned bright red if a guy even asked to borrow a pencil. And now she's in love? No freaking way.

The first bell rings and Sienna links her arm in mine. "C'mon, Tor, I'll tell you all about him on the way to our lockers." I briefly hesitate but then remind myself that this *is* Sienna. Sienna, my best friend since forever. She just looks a whole lot better so it's easy to forget that fact.

And apparently the sad-looking girls we're walking away from would agree. They were probably hoping Sienna would stay and talk more about her trip. Personally, I don't get the sudden attention. Is it because of her new style, the boyfriend development, or her family's recent wealth? All I know is nobody hung on every word of the curly-haired, T-shirt-and-jeans-wearing, single, $1.75-in-her-pocket Sienna of last year. I'm hoping that girl is still in there somewhere.

We walk toward school and Daphne Mason, this girl who made fun of me for wearing knockoff Ugg boots last year, opens the door for us. "Hi, Sienna! Hi, Tori!" she greets us. I give Sienna a questioning look but she's staring straight ahead with a confident smile. A flash of hurt crosses Daphne's eyes, obviously because Sienna didn't respond. I could have girly-squealed and hugged Daphne and she'd have the same look, I'm sure.

Okay, I'll admit it. I'm totally freaking. What's the deal with Sienna? And why did she stop e-mailing me? Because of this Antonio? Maybe she was too busy making out in one of her three bedrooms to type a few words and hit Send.

Part of me wants to yell and demand to know why she stopped writing. Part of me wants to remind her that just because you get a shiny new friend, in this case a boy, you don't go and dump the old one. Like that song we learned in Girl Scouts when we were in second grade about making new friends but keeping the old. How one is silver and the other gold. *I'm* the gold one.

I don't say any of this, however.

We walk through the crowded hallways until we reach the seventh-grade corridor and my new locker, number 142. Sienna leans her back against the locker next to mine and has a dreamy look on her face. I test my new locker combo. A moment later I pop open the door and hang my backpack inside.

"So, how did you meet this guy?" I ask, not sure I'm buying this whole I-have-a-boyfriend thing.

"Oh, it was really great. He was there with his parents for the summer too, staying down the beach a ways. And this one night there was this super lame luau that my parents dragged me to. I was standing near the guys who dig up the cooked pig from the ground and when I looked up Antonio was standing right next to me. He said, 'That's pretty gross.' And I said, 'Yeah. I may go vegetarian.' And he said, 'I'll join you.' And that was it. We hung out every day after that."

"That's, er, romantic. I guess," I say.

"Isn't it though?"

"Did you guys kiss and stuff?"

"Tori!" she scolds, like she wouldn't talk about such things. Like we didn't spend hours in my bedroom last year practice-kissing on our forearms. But then she nods. "We did. He's a great kisser."

"Really? What was it like?"

She waves her hand in the air. "Oh, you know. Awesome."

No. I don't know. She knows that *I* don't know. "Yeah. Sure," I say instead.

Okay, now Sienna's had her first kiss too. If I'm to buy this whole story, that is. So let's review: she ditches me for the summer, doesn't call or write, gets a new boyfriend, has her first kiss, and comes back looking like she should have paparazzi following her. Wait. *Does* she have paparazzi following her? I look around the hallway, eyeing everyone. No. Of course not. I've been frequenting too many celebrity gossip blogs.

"I miss him," Sienna pouts, pursing her pink lips.

"Who?" I ask, caught up in my own thoughts.

"Antonio, of course. Aren't you listening to me?"

"Oh yeah, your new *boyfriend*. Of course. I'm totally listening to you, Sienna. Sorry, I guess I was distracted. I think my jeans are too tight or something." I wiggle my hips and pull at the knees of my jeans.

"Oh." Sienna looks my jeans up and down and slightly wrinkles her nose. "Those are, uh, real cute, Tor."

My jaw drops. No, she didn't. I look down at my jeans. They *are* cute. She totally just dissed my clothes.

Okay, the Sienna of three months ago, my best friend Sienna, the Sienna who wouldn't think twice about going to school in flannel pajama pants, would never make fun of my clothes. How could she have changed so much?

3

It's lunchtime and we (we being not only Sienna and me but *all* of the seventh-grade girls) have basically done nothing today but talk about the fab Sienna, her fab life, and her fab boyfriend. It's getting fabulously annoying.

Sea and I exit the lunch line and carry our full trays to the nearest empty table. It's not the table we sat at last year. Not even close. Last year we sat at one of the farthest tables along the back wall of the cafeteria. The closest ones are always reserved for the cool kids. I guess they can't be bothered to carry their trays too far.

The view is definitely different from up here. It's much brighter and not as cramped. And it's missing that strange smell that always lingered in the back part of the cafeteria—a mix of old dirty mops and the orange powder that janitors sprinkle all over when a kid yaks on the floor.

I look over at our old section of the cafeteria and see Tami and Jenna. We sat with them every day last year. They're both giving me a questioning look—probably wondering what the heck I'm doing up here—so I wave and shrug. Beats me what I'm doing up here. Sienna led the way and took a seat and no one said boo about it. I just followed, which is new in our relationship. Last year Sienna would follow me more. Not that I had great places to go or anything.

I look back at Sea, who is going on and on about something, her fork poised over her plain salad with light Italian dressing. A world of difference from her standard giant-cookie-and-chocolate-milk-shake lunches of the past.

". . . and Antonio said, 'I'll give you another ten if you put her name in the song,' " Sienna is saying.

"That's *so* sweet!" Avery Andrews coos, and the others—Natalie Simmons, Talia Bordecki, and Maya Torreni—*aww* in chorus. "Isn't that the sweetest thing you've ever heard in your whole life, Tori?"

I nod absentmindedly. I've been trying to block out the Antonio-is-wonderful talk since third period. It's been story after nauseating story the entire morning.

I check out Sea's nails while she talks. She used to bite them to the nub but now she has a fancy French manicure with a little rhinestone on each pinkie. She pushes a piece of her satiny hair behind her right ear and tugs the lobe between the knuckles of her index and middle fingers. The smoothness of her hair is a pretty amazing transformation, I must admit. I'd love to know what she's using on it. Probably an eighty-dollar-an-ounce conditioner composed of crushed pearls mixed with oils only found in flowers that grow on a Tibetan mountainside.

"And Antonio said the music was almost as pretty as my voice," Sea continues, pulling on her right earlobe again.

"Wow," Talia breathes, putting a hand over her heart.

Hmph. That's kind of strange. Sienna's been pulling on her ear an awful lot today. It reminds me of when we were kids and this older girl named Molly, who used to hang out at my neighborhood playground, was bragging about her expensive custom-made American Girl doll. Sienna told Molly that she too had an American Girl doll—Samantha was her doll's name, if I remember correctly. Well, there was no Samantha doll. At least, I never saw her. But Sienna would talk about her all the time whenever we were on the playground and Molly was around. Molly would tell Sea to bring her doll along and Sienna would say that she couldn't because Samantha would get dirty. Back then whenever Sea mentioned Samantha she'd pull her right earlobe like that. I totally knew there was no doll, but I didn't want to hurt Sea's feelings so I never said anything.

"Antonio's always telling me to keep talking, just because he likes hearing my voice." Sea giggles and pulls her earlobe again.

I sit bolt upright and stare at Sea, mouth hanging open. Oh my god.

Sea gives me a quizzical look. "What?"

Antonio is like Samantha, as in nonexistent. Ha ha, Sea's boyfriend is fake! Oh wow, this is too much. I have to keep it to myself. For now, anyway. "Um, nothing," I say.

"Have you ever been serenaded?" Maya asks me.

"Oh sure, all the time," I reply without thinking. Wait. What's serenaded?

"Really?" Sienna says, suddenly turning her attention to me.

"Um, yeah," I say. I'm not liking the bit of attitude I'm hearing in her voice.

"Who?"

"Who, what?"

"*Who* serenades you all the time?" she asks.

Sienna is giving me a look like I'm full of it. The other girls are looking at me too, waiting for my response. I glance at the table next to us—a bunch of guys from the seventh-grade football team. They're clowning around, throwing an aluminum foil ball back and forth, and I'm kinda hoping it lands over here. Something to distract all of this attention away from me.

"Well, my, um . . ." I pause. Who? Who serenades me? I have to say something. Wait. I've got it. I sit up straighter and look directly at Sienna. "My boyfriend," I answer matter-of-factly.

"Your boyfriend?" she says, giving me a doubtful look. Like she doesn't believe me. "What boyfriend?"

I smile widely. Why didn't I think of this earlier? If Sienna can make up a fake, conveniently long-distance boyfriend, then I can too. "*My* boyfriend," I say smugly.

Sea narrows her eyes at me. "What's his name?"

I feel like we're in a Ping-Pong match and the other girls are all sitting in the stands watching us volley the ball back and forth.

"Sebastian," I answer quickly. I've always loved that name. I named my first boy Barbie doll Sebastian and I plan on naming a kid Sebastian. If I ever have a kid, that is.

"Sebastian what?" she counters.

Oooh. That's harder. I've never thought about fake

last names. I look off to the side, and into the big window of the kitchen where the lunch ladies are cooking. One of them is pouring a huge pot of boiling water into a metal bowl full of holes. "Colander!" I practically shout, proud of myself for thinking something up so quickly.

"Sebastian Colander?" Sienna says slowly, scrunching up her nose.

"Yes, it's Italian." *For spaghetti strainer,* I think, and stifle a giggle.

"Why are you only mentioning him now?" she asks.

"Well, you've been talking a lot about your trip and Antonio. And I didn't want to brag," I add. Oooh, burn. Okay, normally I wouldn't be trying to zing my best friend but she totally started it. Coming back to school with fake hair, a fake tan, and a fake boyfriend doesn't make you a different person. Maybe just a fake person.

Sienna suddenly has nothing to say. She purses her lips and studies my face, like she's hoping I'll crack and give something away. The girls are eyeing me now too.

"So tell us about Sebastian, Tori," Avery prompts. "Where did you meet him? What's he like?"

"Oh, well, he's perfect. Gorgeous. Funny. Brilliant," I lie, laying it on thick. But hey, as long as I'm going to have a fake boyfriend, I should have a rockin' one, right?

Who makes up a fake boyfriend covered in zits with swamp breath?

Sienna crosses her arms and leans back in her chair.

"We met at art camp," I continue, "in Chicago. Remember that one my mom sends me to for two weeks every July, Sea?"

Sienna nods but still gives me a skeptical look.

"He's in eighth grade, and we were both taking this two-hour landscape class and I accidentally spilled some green paint on his lap, and, well, the rest was history." Okay, that story came rolling out a little too easily.

"Wow. That's *so* romantic, Tori! Why doesn't stuff like this ever happen to me?" Avery whines.

Because you almost failed creative writing last year, I think.

"Seriously, Tori," Natalie pipes in from next to Avery, "you and Sienna both had these great summers and now you both have these awesome boyfriends. You guys should like, double-date or something."

"Yeah, we totally should. Right, Sea?" I briefly smile and then frown. "Oh, but both of our guys live out of town. Shoot. I guess it wouldn't work." I hope my disappointment in this convenient fact is really coming across.

"I guess not," Sienna agrees.

Judging from her expression, it's obvious that this new development is bothering the heck out of her. But there's not a whole lot she can do about it. I guess if she wanted to be the first to hear about Sebastian and me, she should have, I don't know, taken a minute to call me over the summer.

4

I jump off the last step of the afternoon bus and trudge toward my house, fishing for my key in the front of my backpack. Mom won't be home until after five, so I'm on my own until then. Last year at this time Sienna and I would be sitting at my kitchen counter smearing peanut butter on apple slices and swapping stories about who at school had changed the most over the summer and who we thought was cute. But that was last year. I didn't feel like inviting Sienna over today, and anyway, it's not like she stopped and said, "Oh, hey, Tori, my mom can give you a ride back to my house in our big fancy new car and we can play my new Wii and order pizza." Nope. She just climbed into the passenger seat of her car with a casual "IM you later?" tossed over her shoulder. I nodded and boarded the giant yellow bus of gloom.

Once inside, I call Mom to let her know that I got home okay and then pull two tangerines out of the fridge and set them on the counter in front of me. I check the clock. 3:05. I'm already bored. I contemplate going online even though Mom told me I couldn't but then decide against it. She's always a sneaky one with those parent spy programs and she'll just find me out and yell at me later if I do. I consider calling Dad. It's not Sunday or Wednesday, the days we have scheduled calls, but I want to talk to someone, so I pick up the phone and dial.

"Hello?" his warm voice greets me.

"Dad! Hi!" I feel my cheeks pop into a smile.

"Hey, sweetie, everything okay?" He sounds a little surprised to hear from me.

"Yeah, good. I just got home from school," I say.

"Oh that's right, first day today. How'd it go? Was it everything you ever imagined?"

"Oh . . . you know. It was okay."

"That good, eh?" He laughs.

I laugh too. "Yeah. I miss you."

"Well, you're coming up to see me this weekend, right? I'm all set for your visit. I thought we could hit a museum on Saturday and do lunch near the lake. It'll be great."

That does sound great. "Yeah," I answer.

"Wonderful. Well, can we chat more later, hon? I'm kind of covered in paint at the moment."

"Oh, sorry, Dad."

"No problem. I'm glad you called. Love you, sweetie. See you Friday night."

"Love you," I say, and hang up the phone.

Dad's an artist, so he's covered in paint most of the day. He has this great little apartment in Chicago with a view of Lake Michigan from the bedroom. He always lets me have his room when I visit, and I spend a good chunk of the time watching teeny-tiny people walk up and down the bike path lining the lake. Dad's a really, really good painter and has these art shows that important snooty people attend. They talk about lines and strokes while drinking wine and eating cheese cubes. He's not super well-known yet, I guess, but he will be huge someday. I'm sure of it.

I peel my first tangerine and check the clock. 3:10. It's going to be a long afternoon.

Mom comes through the door at 5:15 on the nose with what smells like Chinese food. "Tor? Tori?" I hear her call. I close the book I'm reading and head into the kitchen.

Mom's mascara is smudged under her eyes and she looks tired, but she's smiling anyway. "Well? How was it?" she asks.

Glorious! Stupendous! Best day of my life! All answers she's waiting for. "It was okay," I reply.

"How are your new teachers?" she pushes, setting a paper plate and a bag full of plastic utensils in front of me.

I shrug. "Well, Mr. Matthews has some kind of anger issues. I heard his wife just left him. And Mrs. Wittler kept topping off her coffee with something out of a small silver flask throughout science. I'm thinking whiskey."

"Tori!" Mom scolds, slamming down a carton of beef and broccoli on the kitchen counter.

"What? You asked."

Mom shakes her head in one of those "what am I going to do with her?" ways while scooping some of the beef and broccoli onto her plate.

"Did you catch up with your friends?" she asks. If Mom paid closer attention to me, she'd know my BFFs of late have been Jade, Isabella, and Aubrey, the main characters in the Thornwood Prep books. I read the entire series this summer.

"Yeah."

"How was Sienna's trip? Did she have a great time? Does she look different?" She plucks two egg rolls from a carton, depositing one on my plate.

Ha! She wouldn't believe me if I told her. "Uh-huh," I say. "She had fun."

Mom stops fixing her plate and looks at me and my

mostly empty one. "What's wrong, Tor? Just wiped out from the first day?"

"Yeah, I think so. I'm not hungry. Mind if I go to my room now?" I ask.

"Go ahead, sweetie. We can talk later. Oh! And take your fortune cookie with you. You know you love those." She smiles.

I turn and leave, taking the little cellophane-wrapped cookie with me. I *don't* love fortune cookies. Not at all, actually. There is no chocolate or raisins or any other remotely cookielike goodness to them. Might as well eat a foam cup. I do, however, love the fortunes.

Safely behind my bedroom door, I rip away the plastic wrapper and crack open the crescent-shaped cookie.

> "It is better to be deceived by one's friends than to deceive them."
> —Johann Wolfgang von Goethe

Pssh. That's what he thinks.

5

I toss the cookie and the fortune in the trash and take a seat at my desk in front of my computer. I want to Google this restaurant in Chicago I heard about so Dad and I can go there this weekend. It's something with the word *fondue* in it. I heard you can dip every-thing from pretzels to pickles in the cheese they give you. I *love* cheese. I'm just saying.

Flash. An IM window opens up. Sienna. I glance at my crumpled fortune in the trash can.

SiennasHeart: Hey, Tori
ToritUp: Hey

Doo da doo.
Crickets. Lots of crickets.
Hearing pins drop . . . Well, I have no pins in my

room but I have a pink cup of pens on my desk. I knock the cup over. Hearing pens drop . . .

> **TorItUp:** You IMed?
>
> **SiennasHeart:** ☺ Hey, sorry about that. So, what's up? I didn't get to talk to you much after lunch. How was the rest of your summer?

How was the rest of my summer? *How was the rest of my summer?* Okay, I need to calm down. She's trying here. She wants to know about me.

> **TorItUp:** Really good. Just, you know, hung around and stuff.
>
> **TorItUp:** Spent a week at my dad's after art camp.
>
> **TorItUp:** Marnie Johanson had a pool party. That was fun.
>
> **TorItUp:** Went to Six Flags twice.

Um, distracted much? What, am I talking to myself here?

> **TorItUp:** Are you still there, Sea?
>
> **SiennasHeart:** Sorry! Yeah, I'm here. It's

just Antonio's IMing me too. He's so
funny. He has me LOLing like crazy.

Oh, isn't that special? She's talking to *Antonio*. And
he's *so* funny in addition to being wonderful. Imagine
that. She's just about worn the L and the O right off
her keyboard. Yippee. Why did she IM me then if she's
busy talking to her make-believe boyfriend? Just to
show off? Well, two can play at that game.

> **TorItUp:** Oh, me too. Not IMing with
> Antonio, ha ha, but with my boyfriend.
> Sebastian.
> **SiennasHeart:** Tell him I said hi.
> **TorItUp:** Ok.

Yeah. I'll get right on that. I cross the room to the
silver makeup crate on my bed stand and rummage
through it. Ah, there it is. My Enchanting Espresso
nail polish. I got it one day over the summer when
I was just about to keel over from extreme boredom
and I walked up to the Walgreens at the corner of Wash-
ington and Monroe. I sit back down in front of my PC
and set to work on my nails. Soon I have one hand
finished and I'm blowing on the second coat of my
other hand.

SiennasHeart: Still there, Tori?

I blow on my nails one more time and then carefully type.

TorItUp: Yeah. Sorry. Sebastian was telling
me a story about this kid at his school.
He's SO funny. LOL.

Yeah. I can have a funny fake boyfriend too, Sea.

SiennasHeart: Oh. Well, you probably want
to talk to him. I'll IM you later. Or just
see you at school tomorrow. Bye.

Oh. She signed out. Well, geez. I didn't want to hurt her feelings or anything. I mean, she was talking to her fake boyfriend too. Or pretending to. Whatever. Shoot. Now I feel sorta bad.

6

I kiss Mom's cheek and climb out of her car, ready for another fun-filled day at NJHS. Daphne Mason and Bella Hardy are parked in front of the main doors, examining each other's hairstyles. Both full of silky-smooth, flatiron goodness. I never did get into that. I always heard it takes like an hour to flatiron one's hair and really, what's the point? A little wave never killed anyone. I could be reading or goofing around online during that hour. It's wash and go for me all the way. Well, a brush here and there when I'm really trying.

"Hey, Tori," Daphne says. "Cute top."

I look down at my shirt. Really? It's just a pink "Support cancer research" tee over a long-sleeve white shirt. Free with donation. It's not an expensive fancy-schmancy white tee like Daphne's or anything.

"Uh, thanks," I say. I attempt to walk past the girls,

but Daphne grabs my arm. I look down at her hand and then at her.

"So listen, we were just talking about Wittler. You know, our science teacher? What do you think her story is?" She rubs her hands together and shifts her weight from one foot to the other, like she's waiting for me to really dish it good.

I hesitate. It's not that I don't *want* to talk to these girls. It's only that they've never talked to me before so I have to wonder what their motivation is here. Am I being set up, or are they truly being friendly?

I look at each girl. "You mean with her happy juice?" I finally ask.

Daphne slaps Bella's shoulder, and Bella mouths an "ow."

"I told you, Bella!" Daphne exclaims. "I told you there was something funny in that little silver bottle she has." Daphne looks at me. "She's drinking, right? In class. Right in front of us!"

I shrug. "That's what I thought."

"Oh my gosh, Tori, you totally have to sit by us in science today. We have to get to the bottom of this. I want to know if my teacher is getting sloshed during school," Daphne says.

I raise my eyebrows like I'm mulling it over. "Okay,"

I agree. "See you then." I walk past the girls into school and head to my locker.

So that was kinda weird. Daphne and Bella want me to sit with them? While Bella has never been mean to me like Daphne, she's never gone out of her way to be nice either. I wonder why the change.

Sienna is already standing at my locker, waiting for me. "Hey, Sea. Sorry about cutting you short last night on IM," I say. And I really am. That wasn't me. Not how I am with Sienna, anyway. I mean, she's my only friend. Well, I'm not a leper or anything. I have some "friends." She's just my one truest bestest friend. We've never kept secrets from each other and I've never lied to her. Before now, that is. I guess my feelings are hurt from the summer of ignoration. Is that a word? It totally should be if it's not. I'll have to Google it later.

"Don't worry about it, Tor. I know how it is. Boyfriends require a lot of attention," she says.

Oh. So we're continuing with this then? All righty. "Yep," I agree, "they sure do."

"So listen," Sienna begins, "Lauren and Anica want to walk to the public library after school today to hang out. Can you come?"

Lauren and Anica? As in Lauren Hanson and Anica Speckler? Okay, if Daphne and Bella are "popular," then Lauren and Anica are three levels above that. Most of the seventh-grade girls are afraid to even talk to them. They just stare at them in awe and then try their darnedest to copy their look. I've often thought it would be a fun little social experiment for Lauren and Anica to make a really crazy fashion statement—say, come to school with twenty rainbow-colored ribbons tied throughout their hair—and then see how long it took before the rest of the class was sporting the same style. They're certainly a powerful duo. Which begs the question, Why on earth would they want to sit at a library with us? With me?

"Um, are you sure they want to go with us?" I ask.

Sienna giggles. "Well, yeah. Lauren is really sweet. She's in my history class and we were talking about this one-page assignment due on Friday and she mentioned going to the library today to work on it." Sienna gives me a concerned look. "Do you not want to go?"

"Oh, no. I'll go. I just didn't know, you know, that we were, uh, friendly with them."

Sienna looks relieved. "Oh, yeah. It'll be fun. You can do whatever homework you have. Or go online or whatever."

"Okay. Sounds good," I reply, and we head for homeroom together.

After homeroom, I head for my science class. There, Daphne and Bella wave me over right away. I pass my desk from yesterday and walk toward theirs in the back corner of the room, setting my stuff down at an empty desk next to Daphne's.

My stomach churns a bit and I briefly consider turning back and sitting somewhere else. But that would be way rude at this point.

"We have the *perfect* plan," Bella whispers.

"You know how Wittler has an office back here?" Daphne asks.

I nod. It's practically right behind us.

"I saw her carry that silver bottle in there yesterday."

I think for a moment. "Yeah. You're right. She did do that."

"Well," Daphne continues, "yesterday when Brad Peters got in trouble she sent him to sit in her office for ten minutes. So *I'm* going to get in trouble during class so she sends me too. And I'll just go through her drawers while I'm there and see what she's got."

I smile. "Sounds like a good plan."

A few minutes later class starts and Mrs. Wittler takes roll. She passes out a pop quiz and we all set to work. Mrs. Wittler walks down the aisle between Daphne and me, and we look at each other and then turn to watch her go in her office. Daphne mouths, "Told you." A few moments later Mrs. Wittler returns to the front of the room.

"This is stupid," Daphne announces, breaking the silence. The whole class turns and stares at her.

My stomach does a flip. I know this is the plan, for Daphne to get in trouble, but now that it's happening I'm nervous for her. She sure doesn't look scared though.

"Excuse me?" Mrs. Wittler says, a look of fury across her face. She pulls her glasses down on her nose so that she can glare at Daphne over the top of them. I've often wondered if glasses-wearing adults really need to do this to see or if they do it because they think it fills youths with fear.

"This quiz. It's stupid. It's only the second day of class. How are we supposed to know any of this stuff?"

Oh my god, oh my god, oh my god. This girl is so gutsy. I love it! I'd never ever confront a teacher like this myself, but it's kind of interesting watching her. Not to mention, her question is extremely valid.

Mrs. Wittler looks appalled. And not about to address Daphne's question. "Daphne Mason," she growls, "pick up your things and go sit in my office. Do not come out until your quiz is complete."

The whole class is silent, watching the showdown.

"Whatever," Daphne says, gathering her things. She winks at Bella and me as she pretends to be mad and stomps to Mrs. Wittler's office.

I smile at Bella.

"Tori Barnes, do you have something you wish to share?" Mrs. Wittler asks.

I shake my head.

"Then back to your quiz. Everyone." Mrs. Wittler gives the room the evil eye and then sits on her stool, taking a long sip from her coffee cup.

I wait until Mrs. Wittler is looking down at some work on her lab table before I sneak a look at Daphne in the office. Daphne is laughing and rubbing her hands together. She must have found something good.

"What?" I mouth to her.

She holds up her index finger, so I wait. A moment later she peeks into the room to make sure Mrs. Wittler isn't looking at her and then pulls a giant brown bottle of whiskey from behind her back.

Bella and I look at each other, gaping. Oh my gosh, the teacher is really freakin' drinking during class!

Daphne covers her mouth and her shoulders shake. She darts another look at Mrs. Wittler and then returns to the teacher's desk and puts the whiskey back where she found it.

After we turn in the quizzes and Daphne's punishment ends, she comes back to her seat, slapping hands with Bella and me.

I like these girls. They're fun.

7

The last bell rings and I grab my stuff from my locker and head for the school doors.

"Later, Tori," Daphne calls from her locker down the hallway, and Bella, who is waiting for her, waves.

"Later," I echo. I sling my backpack over my shoulder. It's heavy. It's only the start of the school year and the teachers are already loading on the homework.

"There you are," Sienna says, coming out of the bathroom.

"I was coming to look for you," I reply.

"I was doing a quick makeup check. You need to stop?"

I shake my head. I'm not wearing any makeup, so nope.

"Great, let's go out and meet them," Sienna says.

We walk outside and Lauren and Anica are leaning against the bike rack, waiting for us. Lauren is wearing a purple top, short pink skirt, and long purple slouch boots, and Anica has on almost the same outfit but reversed colors. It's like they just swapped skirts once they got to school.

"Hey," Sienna calls, and the girls smile sweetly. I nod. They're so popular that it feels like coming face-to-face with Carrie Underwood and Kelly Clarkson. The only phrase that comes to mind is "I love your music." But that obviously isn't appropriate for this situation.

We start the four-block walk to the public library, and I'm doing more listening than talking. Lauren is asking Sienna questions about where she stayed this summer. It seems Lauren went to the Keys with her family last year, so they have loads to compare.

When we get to the library we take a seat at a rectangular table in the teen zone. Our library was rebuilt last year, so it's totally decked out. The teen section doesn't only have books—it has a ton of computers, a little café, a media center, and a small stage for performances. It's *the* place to be. Everybody comes here. Even when it wasn't the hot spot, Sea and I came to the library all the time over our summer breaks. One of our favorite things to do was sneak into the adult section and grab a romance novel. They were really easy to spot—we just had to look for covers with guys with long greasy hair and big bare chests, and bingo. We'd stuff them into more age-appropriate books like *Little House on the Prairie* and sit in the children's section reading. We'd giggle and point out the funny parts to each other, like "her heaving bosoms" or "his arched muscular back." It kind of makes me laugh even thinking about it now. I should ask Sea if she remembers.

"So do you miss Antonio?" Lauren asks Sienna.

Or not.

"Oh, so much. It's really hard not being able to see him," Sienna replies.

Uh-huh. I have a hard time not seeing make-believe people too.

"I know what you mean," Lauren commiserates. "Well, not totally, but I only get to see Pete once a week on Saturdays."

I must have a confused look, because a second later Sienna tells me, "Pete is Lauren's boyfriend. He goes to the Catholic school."

"Yeah," Lauren pipes in. "Our parents only allow us one movie a week on Saturday afternoons. My mom drops off and his mom picks up."

"Oh," I say, nodding.

"And I don't even get that," Anica remarks. "I'm going out with Pete's best friend, Evan, but we don't actually ever *go* anywhere. We're allowed one ten-minute phone call a night. But all the time online that we want," she quickly adds. "As long as my mom doesn't catch me, that is."

"So we *all* have boyfriends here," Sienna concludes, smiling.

Yeah. We're a regular boyfriend club. Except Lauren's and Anica's boyfriends sound more real than Sienna's and mine.

"Have you kissed Antonio yet?" Lauren asks Sienna.

Sienna's cheeks actually flush. I'm impressed. I don't think I could make myself flush on the spot like that. Wait, I'm going to try. Nope, nothing.

"Well, yeah," she answers sheepishly.

"Did he ever pass you his gum?" Anica asks.

"Eww," I let out. I can't help it. That's disgusting.

Sienna looks at me. "You mean Sebastian never passed you his gum?"

"Uh, no. That's so gross. Do you know how dirty the human mouth is? I read online somewhere that the human mouth is literally bursting with bacteria. And you want to take someone else's bacteriaed-up gum and put it into your mouth? Pssh. No thanks. Not me."

"What about when he sticks his tongue in your mouth?" Lauren inquires, and Sienna and Anica cover their mouths and giggle.

I shrug. My fake boyfriend's fake tongue doesn't

have any real bacteria on it, so I've never found it to be a problem.

Sienna suddenly stands, breaking up the conversation. "Hey, Tori, wanna go with me to check e-mail?"

"Sure," I reply, grateful for the escape. I get up and follow her.

We sign in at the librarian's desk and then take seats at two of the computers. I launch a Web browser and check my e-mail.

"Oh!" Sienna squeals with delight.

"What's up?" I ask.

"Look, Antonio wrote me this long e-mail and it's *so* sweet."

I glance over and read:

To: SiennasHeart@funmail.com
From: Antonio.Rodriguez@funmail.com
Re: Your day

Hey Sienna,
How's your day? What are you—

Sienna slaps a hand across the screen. "Wait. I better read it first. I don't know what the rest of it says." She turns the monitor away from me and reads.

So it's like that? Well, two can set up fake e-mail accounts.

I quickly log myself out and set up a new account for one SColander.

"Awwww . . ." Sienna moans from beside me, and I throw her a glare.

Once the account is set up, I decide not to write myself an e-mail but to do something a little grander. I log on to kiss2u.com and scan the available kisses for a good one.

"AWWWW . . ." Sienna remarks, louder now, pouting out her bottom lip and wiggling her shoulders.

She's really going for the Golden Globe here.

I select the "Thinking of You" kiss and type my e-mail address in the To: box and Sebastian's in the From: box, add a cute message, and click Send.

Sienna lets out a dramatic happy sigh and glances at me, obviously disappointed that her audience isn't paying attention. "What are you doing?" she asks.

"I'm just about to check my e-mail," I reply. I make a big production of opening my e-mail in a new window. "Oh, look. A kiss."

"What?" Sienna asks. She scoots over to look at my screen.

I launch my e-kiss. "Aww . . . look at that, Sea. Isn't it *so* cute? You see? The big kiss is thinking about the little kiss in the thought bubble. And there's a message: 'I'm thinking about you all the time.' Oh!" I place my hand over my heart and wink really hard, trying to squeeze out a tear or two of joy. But I've got nothing. I should really practice this stuff at home first.

I look at Sienna, and her lips are drawn tight and her eyes are narrowed. I think she may be jealous.

I smile and sing in my head, *My fake boyfriend is better than yours.*

8

It's been a long first week of school, and I've been doing the "thank God it's Friday" chant since I woke up this morning. I can't wait for the school day to pass so I can get to Dad's. I really need a break. I don't know about real boyfriends, but fake boyfriends are exhausting. I mean, there is a lot required to keep a relationship going and thriving. This week alone I had two imaginary marathon phone calls with Sebastian, I fake-baked and mailed him a batch of his favorite M&M cookies (using only handpicked blue M&M's; it's his favorite color and I'm thoughtful like that), and I had to make a big deal out of the oooey-gooey love note he e-mailed me. Avery had me read it aloud to the lunch table *three* times yesterday. Honestly, I don't know how people with real boyfriends keep up with them *and* go to school at the same time. I may wait to date a real boy until I'm out of high school. Well . . . I don't want to get carried away or anything. If I get a living breathing boyfriend someday, maybe I'll have to lighten my class load.

Mom had another meeting this morning, so she dropped me off at school early. I'm the first one in homeroom. I know I should have waited outside for Sea to get here, but frankly, hanging out with her this week has been a bit exhausting too. There is only so much of the Antonio-is-Mr.-Wonderful talk a girl can take. According to Sienna, if the boy burps the heavens sing. His voice can melt chocolate for fondue. He doesn't own a comb or mirror because he wakes up beautiful. Brilliance leaks from his pores.

Okay, maybe she didn't exactly say those things, but close enough. And the kids in this school suck it up like a vacuum. It's like they don't have enough drama in their own lives so they want to hear all about Sienna's. Maybe they need to watch more TV.

Oh sure, people want to hear about my darling Sebastian too; I do spin a good tale. But I'm a pale light next to Sienna's star. She's the main attraction this school year. I'm merely the Gayle to her Oprah.

Not that I'm complaining. Much. It's not *awful* having these new friends. Daphne and Bella are a blast, and Avery and the lunch crew are nice enough. Lauren and Anica seem sweet and amusingly color-coordinated in their daily outfit choices. But things weren't awful before either. It's not that I didn't want more friends; I just didn't seem to need them. I always had Sea, and that was enough for me. But maybe it wasn't for her.

I might feel different if I thought these girls liked me for me and not because I'm Sienna's phone-a-friend. The only reason they are hanging all over us is that they're drawn to Sea like to a giant tub of buttery popcorn—they can't help but want a little. But take away all the butter and salt, and would the popcorn still taste as good?

Whoa. I think I'm getting a little too philosophical for 7:30 in the morning. And a little hungry. I forgot to eat breakfast.

I reach into my backpack and pull out an oatmeal bar. As I'm ripping it open, Sienna strolls in with Avery and Natalie close behind.

"Morning, Tori," Sienna calls, and Avery and Natalie echo their hellos.

I raise my eyebrows and wave, my mouth full of oatmeal bar.

"I thought you were going to wait for me," Sienna comments in a slightly whiny voice.

I wipe crumbs from my mouth. "Sorry. I was up late. I'm still trying to wake up."

"It's all right. I hung out with Avery and Natalie outside."

Uh, that's nice. I smile halfheartedly.

"Yeah, we were there, so you don't need to worry," Avery says, like she's reassuring me.

Okay, wait. Since when does Sienna need an entourage to get in and around school? And why would I be worried?

Avery and Natalie are giving Sienna dumb smiles, and suddenly I feel a wave of something. Almost like I'm being threatened. Like I should growl at the girls or mark my territory (not literally of course. Eww).

"So, Sea, did you talk to Antonio last night?" I inquire.

Yeah, I actually went there and asked about her fake boy. Something about the way the girls are looking at Sea made me feel like I had to throw my best-friend weight around. Get her attention back on me. Remind them who's who around here.

"I did!" She smiles, obviously delighted for the opportunity to bring him up again. "We were talking about this one night when we were strolling along the boardwalk and saw this crazy guy jumping around on this long green park bench and yelling religious stuff at people passing by. Antonio asked if I got a picture of him and—"

"Pictures?" Natalie squeals and claps her hands. "Do you have pictures of you and Antonio? Oh my gosh, Sienna, you have to show us a picture of him!"

Sienna turns white. Like, literally turns white. I've read in books where people turn white and I always thought they were exaggerating, but nope, Sea is a marshmallow.

"Yeah, I'd love to see a picture too," I say, unable to hide the glee from my face.

"Oh, well, yeah. No problem. It's just they, you know, the vacation photos, are all, um, on my mom's digital camera. And, well, she's going to take them to the drugstore and get them developed. So, after that, you know, I'll bring in some pics." Sienna nods, like she's approving her own story.

Mr. Cooper, our homeroom teacher, walks into class and flips the TV on. Much to Sienna's relief, I'm sure. Every morning we watch *Channel One News* while Mr. Cooper takes attendance to make sure no one is skipping homeroom and having fun. Today the student reporter is talking about a couple of teens that got to be veterinarians for the day at the Brookfield Zoo. I try to appear interested in the dorky-looking kid with the monkey hugging his neck and giving him wet, slobbery kisses.

Sea leans across the aisle and whispers, "What about you? Got a picture of Sebastian?"

Without taking my eyes away from the TV, I whisper back, "You know I don't have a camera."

Sienna makes a *hmph* sound and leans back in her chair, fixing her eyes on the screen. I inwardly smile.

A few minutes later the bell sounds, ending homeroom. We scoot toward the door to get to first hour.

"Hey, did I show you guys the cute bracelet my mom bought me to celebrate the end of the first week of school?" Avery asks. She juts out her wrist, and we look at the thin silver bracelet with the tiny red apple charm dangling from it. It's sweet, if you like fruit jewelry.

"That's *so* cute!" Sienna exclaims. "Antonio sent me a bouquet of carnations to mark the end of the first week of school."

"That's nice," I comment, stepping in front of Sienna and heading out the door. I call back over my shoulder, "Sebastian sent me roses."

9

My train pulls into Union Station and I wait near the doors, anxious to get out. Train people always weird me out a little. Today, for example, the lady next to me was putting her baby-powder-scented deodorant on right there in front of everyone as if this was a perfectly normal thing to be doing on a train. Personally, I do that kind of thing at home and not in front of fifty strangers. I never tell Mom about the weird people on the train though. If I did she'd probably flip out and not let me take the train by myself to see Dad anymore. She figures it's safe enough because she always puts me on at the station by our house in the burbs and Dad meets me at Union Station. And she always reminds me not to make eye contact with anyone on the way here. I don't think eye-to-armpit contact counts.

I jump off the last train, step onto the platform, and scan the crowd looking for Dad. There are people rushing all around me, and for a second I flash back to when I was six and got lost at the county fair. I felt small and helpless back then. But I don't now. Even if Dad wasn't here to meet me, I could find my way around easily. I've walked to his apartment plenty of times. It's just four blocks east on Adams.

"Tori!" Dad yells, jogging toward me.

I swing around and jump into his arms. "Dad! I missed you!" His hair is a little longer than the last time I saw him, and I don't think he's shaved in a few days. Otherwise he looks exactly the same.

"I missed you too, sweetie!" he says. "How was the train ride?"

"Fine. I'm glad to finally be here." I give Dad another quick hug. It's only been a month since my last visit with him, but a month is so long. I miss him all the time. It's been a little over three years now since he and Mom divorced and he moved to the city.

"Here, give me your bag and let's get out of here," he says.

I hand him my backpack and we board the escalator, heading for street level. We exit on Adams, and there are people rushing around in various directions. It's warm out, and the sun is sitting low in the sky.

Dad's chatting away as we walk, pointing out the store where he bought his new fall jacket, talking about an art show he went to last weekend, and waving to the friendly pretzel vendor he discovered who makes "the best soft pretzels on Earth." I nod and smile in the right spots as he goes on and on. I like listening to him talk. I walk fast, trying to match his pace.

"I'm sorry, hon, I've been talking the whole time. Tell me about you. How was your first week of school? How does it feel to be a seventh grader?"

"Oh, it was . . . fine. Seventh grade is different," I say.

Dad nods. "Ah, yes. I can still remember seventh grade. Not the underlings anymore but not running the school either. It's a good grade."

I smile. "Yeah, it's all right." I'm hoping that's the end of the questioning. I kind of want to forget about the week right now. Forget about everything.

"Seventh grade is one of those years," Dad continues, looking wistful, "when anything can happen. You're still trying to figure out who you are before you get to high school. Me? I was quite the stunner back then." He looks down at me smugly.

"You were?" I ask.

"H-U-N-K," he replies. "Ever hear the name Wanda Stolzer?"

I shake my head. "Who's that?"

"Only the most popular girl at Kennedy Junior

High the year I was in seventh grade. Maybe even in all of Kennedy Junior High history. And she was *hot* for my bod."

"Dad!" I groan, covering my ears. I drop my hands back down right away though. A Dad story is exactly what I need to forget my troubles for a while. Dad's face lights up as he talks.

A few minutes later, we're in front of Dad's building.

"Yep," he concludes, "those were the days. A time when a guy could woo a girl based solely on the merit of his robot dance."

I smile and Dad throws an arm around my shoulder and opens the front door to the building with his free hand. "Come on," he says. "Let's get you inside. You want takeout tonight?"

"Sure," I reply, realizing that I am getting pretty hungry. And the takeout by Dad's apartment is always *so* good. It's somehow better than takeout at home.

An hour later we're watching a movie and eating soup and sandwiches from the deli around the corner. Me: cream of broccoli and a turkey and cheddar on wheat. Dad: cream of tomato and an Italian grilled cheese. We're both staring at the TV screen and eating in silence, except for when I start in on my soup. I'm a slurper.

I'm trying to concentrate on the movie, but my mind keeps wandering back to Sienna and how much she's changed in such a short amount of time. And it's not just that she's got a new look, a new "boyfriend," and loads of new friends. It's also that I'm wondering where *we* stand now. Does she still think *I'm* her best friend? Maybe now that she's rich she thinks she's too good for me and just hasn't figured out a way to cut me loose yet. It's hard to believe that this Sienna is the same girl who saved my butt in first grade when the evil Mrs. Kirk made me stand up and spell *house* in front of the entire class. I was stalled after the *o*, debating whether or not *w* came next, when Sea whispered "u-s-e" from behind me and I spelled the word correctly. I have to believe that *that* Sea is in there somewhere and only temporarily confused from inhaling too much hair bleach or something.

Dad reaches for a napkin and wipes his mouth. He picks up the TV remote and hits Pause. "Okay," he states, turning to face me on the couch. "What's going on?"

"What?" I ask. I pull a tiny piece of bread off of the top of my sandwich and put it in my mouth.

"Something's wrong. You're a little off tonight. Did you get in a fight with your mom?"

"No. Mom's fine."

"Got a crush on a boy and he doesn't even know you're alive?"

I giggle. "No . . ."

"Your teachers are all mean and out to get you?"

"Daaaaad!"

"Okay, okay." He put his hands up in surrender. "Want to just tell me what's bugging you?"

"Nothing. Nothing is really bugging me. I told you, I missed you. I'm happy to be here." I try to sound convincing.

"And I'm happy you're here too." He reaches over and ruffles my hair. "But if you decide that you want to tell me about 'nothing,' I'm a really good listener. It was my major in college. I got all A's."

I roll my eyes and laugh. "You're so goofy, Dad."

"Really? I always felt more like Donald than Goofy," he replies, and I groan.

"Come on, hit Play," I tell him, and dip my sandwich into my soup.

The next morning Dad peeks into his bedroom, where I'm staying. "You almost ready to go?" he asks.

I walk around the room checking out his latest artwork. I'm super impressed. Sometimes it's hard to see your parents as these real people who can have talents like Dad so obviously does.

"Dad, these are really *really* good! Are they going to be in your next show?"

"You like them?" He pulls a hand through his wavy brown hair. He always gets a little shy when I see his paintings.

"Uh-huh, a lot," I reply. The walls of his bedroom are lined with painting after painting of people who work around the city. There is one of a CTA bus driver looking down and out of the window at the traffic, another of a baker putting up a box of macaroons on a counter, and another of a commuter sitting on the train, listening to her iPod. I stop in front of one of the paintings, recognizing the smile. "Hey, is this that pretzel guy you pointed out yesterday?"

Dad laughs. "Yeah, that's Max. Do you like it?"

I nod. "The salt on the pretzels looks so real I almost want to lick it."

"Well, don't do that. I got bagels so we can eat before we head out to the museum."

"Mmmm, yum," I comment.

An hour later we're walking up the steps of the Museum of Science and Industry. It was just a quick bus ride to Lake Shore Drive from Dad's. He's so lucky, getting to live near so many cool places. The closest museum to our house is the teacup museum, and really, who wants to spend an afternoon looking at teacups? Not me.

Once inside, we pass right by the guy handing out museum maps. We've been here dozens of times, so you could say we're pros.

"Where to first, my dear?" Dad asks.

I glance at the elevator.

"Straight to the top then?" he says.

"Yes!"

A few minutes later we are walking around the You! The Experience exhibit, looking for the new giant heart. There used to be a sixteen-foot walk-through heart that I loved to run in and out of when I was little. Dad has dozens of pictures of me standing in front of it from over the years. The new heart is much cooler though; you can make it beat with your own.

We reach the heart and I look at Dad and smile.

"Okay, okay. Hold still a sec," he directs.

I put my hands on my hips and grin. Dad snaps a picture with his camera phone.

Next we go to the prenatal development section of the exhibit. It's this long wall of babies, *real babies*, from the different stages of gestation. From a teeny-tiny little embryo all the way up to a fully formed baby. The babies here passed away from one thing or another back in the

1930s, and I guess their parents must have donated their bodies to the museum. I've seen it more times than I can count, but it always freaks me out a bit each time. I'm not sure if I'm more freaked out by the fact that they were once living or by the fact that this is what a baby growing inside a woman looks like. Seriously, the school system could skip the sex education lecture in fifth grade and bring kids here and show them what happens if they're not careful.

I step up to the display case and look at the first few babies. I don't stay freaked out for long. Mostly because Dad always makes me laugh.

"Ah, yes. I remember when you were just a speck. I swore if you never grew another centimeter I'd carry you around just like that. If that big storybook elephant, Horton, could do it, well then so could I." Dad nods for emphasis.

"Dad!" I scold, but then I giggle.

We move to another case and peer in.

"The good ol' tail days," Dad says. "Yours was quite a cute one as I recall, and I'm not only saying that because I'm your father. Your mother worried that it might be there forever, and I said, So what? If our child has a tail, then we'll teach her to be proud of it!"

I shake my head, laughing. "You're so crazy, Dad!" I say, though really I like it when he tells stories about him and Mom, things they said or did when they were still together. When Dad lived with Mom and me in the suburbs, we would drive down to this museum every New Year's Day. It was sort of our family tradition. But then one year we didn't go on New Year's, and the next year Dad moved out. I don't think Mom has even been back to the museum since. But Dad and I go a lot, so I guess Mom sees no reason to. We continue walking along the wall, and any fears I had of the babies have disappeared and my fascination has completely taken over, as it always does.

Next, we head straight down to the fairy castle, this monster huge dollhouse that looks like an enchanted castle that Cinderella would live in if she was real. And five inches tall. It's visually stunning, and I've always thought it a mad waste that it is locked up under the glass case, where no one can play with it. The castle was always Mom's favorite exhibit, and she used to say she'd make me a little one someday. But I'm sure she's forgotten that too by now.

From watching other people here, I find that most museum visitors are boring and look at everything on one floor before moving to the next. But not us. We go in order of our favorite exhibits to least favorite, so we tend to bounce all over the museum. Dad says it's good exercise.

We go up one floor to Yesterday's Main Street and walk along the brick and cobblestone streets in 1910 Chicago. We window-shop at the old stores, watch a short silent movie in the cinema, and stop at the old-fashioned ice cream parlor for a vanilla cone. Then it's straight back to the top floor of the museum to see the transportation section.

I climb aboard the once-in-commission United Boeing 727 airplane, the only real airplane I've ever been on, and take a seat. It's suspended from the ceiling by some super heavy-duty wires, so it's sort of like we're flying. Except we're not moving. There is a real cockpit up front and everything. A minute later Dad sits down beside me and buckles in.

"So what's today's in-flight movie?" he asks.

I groan.

"I have to take you on a trip somewhere soon," he adds, gripping the armrests. "On a real plane. One with an engine."

"Engines are good," I mutter.

I look out the small plane window into the museum. I wonder if this is like the plane Sienna took on her family vacation to the Keys. I wonder if she saw a movie on it. She didn't tell me about the plane ride. She hasn't really talked about anything on the trip that didn't involve Antonio.

"Come on, what's wrong, sweetie?" Dad urges.

"Hmm?" I raise my eyebrows.

"Something's obviously bothering you. Spill."

I hesitate. "It's just . . . Sienna. She changed so much over the summer. Everything is different about her. It's like I don't even know her anymore."

Everything that has been going on with me and Sea over the past week comes flooding out. Dad doesn't say a word while I'm talking but listens and nods occasionally. When it's all out I feel a wave of relief.

"Well, I'm pretty good with these things, Tor. After all, I majored in friendship in college," he starts.

"You said you majored in listening," I interrupt.

"I double-majored. But anyway, I think Sienna must be feeling like she needs to be this different, more fantastical person at school for some reason. I think if you get her away from school and somewhere familiar, like, say, the house, then she'll go back to normal. Why don't you ask Mom if you can have Sienna for a sleepover or something?"

"Dad! You're brilliant!" I throw my arms around his neck and squeeze tight. Of course! She's only acting like this for other people. She won't act like this when it's just her and me.

"Obviously, darling daughter. One has to be brilliant to keep up with you."

10

Pop quiz!" Mrs. Wittler announces Monday morning in science class. "Clear everything off of your desk 'cept for a pencil." Mrs. Wittler's clothing selection today is a bit more on the lax side than last week's. She's wearing a black and silver pin-striped shirt, misbuttoned by one button all the way down, a navy blue lightweight cardigan, and brown poofy pants that taper in at the ankles.

"Shut. Up," Daphne says to me. "Seriously? She just gave us a pop quiz last week. What is she starting, another bad habit?"

Bella snickers and covers her face with her notebook. I grin.

"Somethingz funny, ladies?" Mrs. Wittler sniffs really hard and rubs her nose.

"Of course not, Mrs. Wittler," Daphne replies in a syrupy-sweet voice.

"Is it abnormally hot in here?" Mrs. Wittler asks nobody in particular, waving a hand in front of her face. Her cheeks are pink.

No one says a thing.

"Get out yer pencils! C'mon then," Mrs. Wittler says.

The students pass looks back and forth, but everyone clears their desks and takes out pencils.

"Geez, what does she have, a wedgie or something?" Daphne mumbles. It's too much for us. Bella and I dissolve into a pile of giggles.

"Girls!" Mrs. Wittler yells at us, and my back stiffens. "That's strike . . ." She pauses and rubs her bottom lip with her thumb and index finger like she can't remember how many times she's yelled at us today. "Let's say strike two," she finally says, holding two fingers in the air in a shaky peace sign. "One more and yer outta here!"

Daphne glares at Mrs. Wittler and mumbles under her breath. "Now she's an umpire." I look down at my notebook, concentrating on the swirl of the *T* in my name on the cover. I can't get in any more trouble today for laughing.

I busy myself looking for a pencil. I take out an extra so I don't have to get up during the quiz and sharpen. I don't even care about the pop quiz today. I'm in too good a mood. I had a fantastic weekend with Dad, and I already talked to Sea this morning about having a sleepover at my house this Friday night, just the two of us. It'll be like old times, like the sleepovers we used to have before the summer and everything changed. She said it was a great idea and that she was totally in the mood for a girls' night. Things will be back to normal in no time.

Twenty minutes later, the last student has turned in his quiz and we're waiting for Mrs. Wittler to say something. She's been sitting up in the front of the room at her lab table, both hands wrapped around her mug, sucking down her coffee and staring off into space the whole time.

I reach down to pick up my stuff off the floor and hear a rumble and a curse.

"Oh my god," Bella whispers. "Did you see that? She just stumbled. She's loaded!"

"Kyle Anthony, why're your things in the middle of the aisle? I coulda got hurt." Mrs. Wittler is staring down at Kyle with wild eyes, her hands on her hips.

"But, Mrs. Wittler, they weren't," Kyle says.

"So I'm lying? Zthat what yer saying?"

Daphne leans over to me. "Look at her eyes. They're totally red."

I squint, studying Mrs. Wittler's eyes. I guess they *are* sorta red. I suppose she could have allergies or something too. But I highly doubt it.

"Open your books to, um, page ten," Mrs. Wittler

says. She widens her eyes and squints a couple of times, like she's trying hard to focus on the words.

We open our books to a picture of a plant, and Mrs. Wittler reads the paragraph at the top of the page.

"Did you hear that?" Daphne hisses. "She totally slurred *photosynthesis*! I can't believe she's drunk again."

"Me neither," I whisper.

Daphne watches Mrs. Wittler for a second and then leans toward Bella and me. "We have to report her to Principal Brown."

"I don't want to get in trouble," Bella announces.

"No. None of us will get in trouble. We can do it anonymously. Wednesday night is pizza night at my house. Come over for dinner and we'll make a plan," Daphne replies.

I smile and nod. Bella gives a thumbs-up.

I'm running late for lunch on Wednesday. Actually, I'm the last kid in the lunch line, which is never a good thing. It's hard to take a fruit cup knowing that any one of the hundred kids who passed by it before me could've flung a booger into it. I put a plastic-wrapped turkey sandwich and a bag of chips on my tray and head for our lunch table. Sienna is already there chatting with Natalie, Avery, and Maya.

I catch the tail end of Sienna's sentence as I sit down. ". . . prefers cherry."

"Sebastian likes banana," I say, confident that there's a 99.9 percent chance she's talking about Antonio and not wanting to miss any opportunity of bringing Sebastian into the conversation too.

"Really?" Sea scrunches up her nose. "Where do you find banana lip gloss?"

Oh. We're talking about lip gloss. "Well, I special-order it online. Since he likes it so much and all. I call him my little monkey, heh heh."

"That's so sweet!" Natalie squeals. "I love pet names."

Tori — 1, Sienna — 0

"Do you guys have pet names too, Sienna?" Avery asks.

"Well, uh . . ." Sea hesitates. "Not really, I guess."

"You totally should," I say. "Not that I'm a relationship expert or anything, but I find it gives us an extra special connection, you know?" If anyone would understand how special the connection with your fake boyfriend is, it would be Sea.

Sea doesn't say anything. She looks momentarily uncomfortable and concentrates on her yogurt cup, scraping at the bottom. Avery, Natalie, and Maya start talking about this morning's dance practice. They're on the squad together. I briefly try to look interested in what they're saying, but even I can't fake that. I wouldn't know a floor combo from a mambo.

Sea scoops up the last bit of her yogurt and examines my lunch tray. "Hey, it's pizza day and you didn't get a slice. Are you on a diet or something?"

"Me? Diet? When have you ever known me to reject food? Nah. I'm having pizza tonight at Daphne's, so I thought I'd skip it for lunch."

"Oh. You're going to Daphne's?" Sea blinks at me, and her bottom lip pouts out.

She's jealous. Sheesh. I feel bad now. Like I shouldn't have other friends or go anywhere without her or something. Which I guess I could sorta see. She *is* the reason I have the new friends.

"It's not like we're *friend* friends," I say, trying to make her feel better. "I mean, I don't know them very well or anything. I would totally rather hang out with you, but you said you had that Skype date with Antonio tonight, right?"

Sea looks confused.

"You told me this morning that you and Antonio were going to watch a movie and chat at the same time over Skype. Remember?" Oh my god, there's no date. Well, duh, logically I *knew* there was no date since Antonio is fake and all, but ugh, sometimes this real boyfriend/fake boyfriend stuff gets so confusing. I forgot Antonio wasn't real for a moment.

"Oh, yeah, you're right. I almost forgot," she says.

Oh, man. She didn't even remember that she had an online date tonight. Now she's going to be sitting home alone feeling bad while I'm having fun with Daphne and Bella. I need to give her an out so she can come hang out with us and forget this fake date nonsense.

"Sea, maybe Antonio and you can do your date on another night? That way you can come with me. It'll be fun!" There. That was very nice of me. Very mature. I pretended Antonio was real and I'm giving her the chance to break her fake date and hang with us rather than admit she's been lying about him since day one.

Sienna thinks about my offer, then finally replies, "Nah. I better keep my date. I really miss Antonio, and I know he's been looking forward to our date too."

I try to smile, but in my head all I can hear is *Argh!* She is so frustrating with this stuff.

11

"Thanks for the ride, Mom," I say as we pull into Daphne's driveway. Her house is a small brick split-level with lots of big oak and maple trees in the front yard. The kind I used to climb up into on spring afternoons and read a book in until the sun went down. When I was much younger, of course. I'm too old for tree-climbing now.

"No problem, sweetie," Mom replies. "It's good to see you making new friends." She puts the car in park.

"Um, whatcha doing?"

"Coming in to meet Mrs. Mason, of course."

"Mo-om," I groan. "Don't embarrass me."

"When have I ever embarrassed you?" she asks.

I raise one eyebrow and stare at her, not blinking.

"All right, all right, I won't embarrass you. Come on."

I follow Mom up Daphne's cracked sidewalk and hang back while she rings the doorbell. I turn around and stare up into the leaves of a giant maple tree. They'll be turning a pretty orange soon. The tree reminds me of the time when Sea and I were in fourth grade and were at my house making leaf rubs. We collected all kinds of leaves and sat at the kitchen counter with colored pencils and pieces of paper. We put the paper over different leaves and colored over them with the pencils, lightly, until the imprint of each leaf appeared on the paper.

Sienna was looking out the window and said she spotted *the* perfect leaf at the top of our old maple in the front yard. I don't know what was so special about it—they all looked the same to me. But she *had* to have it. We went outside, and I watched Sea climb to the top of the tree and snatch the leaf from its branch. And then proceed to *freak out*. Her face went pale and she hugged the branch closest to her. At first I giggled because she looked so darn funny up there. But soon I realized she wasn't playing and wouldn't be coming down on her own.

I didn't know what to do, so I did the first thing that came to my mind. I climbed up there after her.

"Sea, come on," I said when I reached her. "I'm right behind you. Start making your way back down."

"No! I can't move. We're too high," she said.

"Sea, you've got to move. We can't live in this tree forever. Well, if we were squirrels we could. But even then we'd have to climb down for nuts. Unless you made me do the nut gathering. Though I don't want that kind of living situation where I'm the one doing all the work. It wouldn't be fair."

"Tori!" Sea yelled in a shaky voice. "Don't make me laugh. I'll lose my grip."

"Well, don't go and do that. I'm underneath you and you'll squash me," I said.

"Tori!" Sea let out a small giggle.

I reached my hand up over my head. "Come on. Grab my hand. You know I have the grip of an orangutan so I'm not going to fall. I'll help you down."

Sea considered this and then nodded. "Okay, but don't let go." She peeled her left hand away from the branch and reached down. I grabbed it.

We proceeded down the tree. It was *really* difficult considering her position right over my head, but I never let go of her hand and we didn't fall. And once we were on the ground, Sea swore she was never climbing another tree for as long as she lived.

"Tori!" a giddy voice squeals.

I turn around, startled. "Hey, Daphne." I break into a big smile.

"Are you coming in? Your mom is in the living room talking to my mom. You were just standing out here, staring at my tree."

I shrug and follow her inside. "Yeah, I like trees."

Ten minutes later I'm sitting cross-legged on Daphne's pink bedspread in her bedroom. Giggling. It's funny how comfortable I am here with them when only last year they never would have talked to me.

"Oh, you loved it!" Bella says, playfully slapping Daphne's shoulder.

"I did not," Daphne says, indignant. Then suddenly she breaks out in a grin. "Okay, you're right. I loved it!" The three of us are laughing now. "You would too, though! Don't lie!"

"Duh," Bella returns. She's referring to earlier today when Joshua Neville tripped in the library and landed right in Daphne's lap. Joshua is an eighth-grade foreign exchange student with a fantastic French accent. Most of the girls think he's cute, but he just keeps to himself. I don't think his English is all that great.

"So how are we going to expose Wittler?" Daphne asks, getting down to business.

"We could wait until the next time she's drunk in class, ask for a hall pass to the bathroom, and go get the principal," I say. "Then she could see for herself."

Bella shakes her head. "Nope. I don't want anyone finding out we snitched."

"But they won't," I protest.

"Bella's right," Daphne agrees. "People will put two

and two together and know it was whoever left the room last. No, we have to give Principal Brown proof but without her knowing it comes from us."

"Like an anonymous letter?"

"Yeah," Daphne says. "But not a letter. She might not believe a letter. We have to give her good, solid proof."

I cross my arms and think. "If only we could figure out how." The room is quiet, and I can hear the numbers on the old digital alarm clock on the nightstand flip.

Daphne suddenly sits up straighter, a grin spreading across her face. "Bella, your brother still works at Anderson's Groceries, right?"

Bella nods.

Daphne rubs her hands together. "I think I've got it."

12

I pull back the living room curtains and peek out the window for the tenth time in the last five minutes. Sienna's mom should be dropping her off any minute now for our sleepover. Mom's in her room reading a book. She's been really great. She bought all of our old favorite things—frozen pizza, potato chips and dip, and a roll of cookie dough. Yeah, I know Sea hasn't been eating anything but bird food lately, but once she sees our old favorites I'm sure she'll cave in and have some. I also pulled our favorite Lindsay Lohan DVDs off the entertainment center shelf for us to watch. Sea and I love Lindsay's old movies but would never admit that to anyone else. I figure it's one more thing to remind Sea that *I* am her best friend and *I* know the real her. Dad's right—tonight everything is going to go back to real: pre–Keys vacation, pre–hair extensions, and pre–fake boyfriends.

I peek out the window again and see Sienna's mom's shiny new Beemer pull into the driveway. "She's here!" I yell to Mom, and swing open the door.

Sienna gives her mom a quick kiss on the cheek, jumps out of the passenger door, and runs up my front walk. Even though we're just having a girls' night, Sienna looks completely adorable. She's got her glossy hair up in a high pony, and she's wearing hot pink and black layered tees and black yoga pants with some pink lettering on the butt. I'm wearing my dad's Art Institute of Chicago T-shirt, circa 1980, and a pair of his old flannel boxers, circa I didn't care to ask. They are comfy, and I found them in the back of his old dresser drawer like six months after he moved out.

I push open the screen door with a big smile. "Sea!" I exclaim. "Yay, I'm so glad you're here. We're going to have *so* much fun tonight!"

Sea gives her mom a final wave over her shoulder and comes into the house.

"Hi, Sienna," Mom says. She must have just walked into the room. "How are you, honey? You look wonderful. Did you have a nice vacation?"

Oh good lord, I think. *Please, oh please, don't get her started on her vacation.*

"Thank you, Mrs. Barnes. And I did have a wonderful vacation. We stayed in this amazing house that had eighteen bedrooms. Eighteen! I had three to my-self alone . . ."

Too late.

About twenty minutes later and three very loud and obnoxious yawns from me in an attempt to signal Mom to return to her bedroom and her reading, Mom finally excuses herself.

"Have fun, girls. I'll be in my room if you need me. Stay in the house and don't prank-call people or chat with any weirdos online, okay? Do you need help with the oven?"

I roll my eyes. Is she serious? This from the woman who makes me bake the Christmas cookies for the neighbors each year. "We're fine, Mom."

She nods and leaves. I turn to Sea and ask, "So what should we do first? Movie? Snacks? Makeovers?"

"I'm so in the mood for a movie," Sea replies. "I tried to watch that one with Antonio the other night, but he wanted to talk through the whole thing."

Blech. Antonio. I need to try harder. "Hey, how about I throw that pizza in too? Then we can eat while we watch the movie. Remember that time last year when you were laughing so hard during a movie that a little piece of pepperoni flew out of your nose?" I giggle.

Sienna gasps and grabs her nose. "Oh my god! You're

right. That stung too," she says, and starts laughing with me. "I couldn't eat pepperoni for like two weeks after that."

"Yeah, well, I had the visual burned into my brain. I still can't eat pepperoni pizza. We've got plain cheese tonight."

"Cheese sounds great to me. Let's make it."

Soon the pizza is ready, so we bring it into the living room and plop onto the floor to watch *Mean Girls*. We've seen it so many times that we take turns reciting the lines along with the actors.

When there are only two slices left and the credits are rolling, Sienna turns to me. "What do you want to do now?"

I think. "Um, how about facials?"

"Oh, I *love* facials! I had this awesome sugar scrub facial on vacation . . ."

No. No, no, no, we are not talking any more about her vacation! I cut her off. "A sugar scrub sounds easy. Let's go to the kitchen and see what we've got."

Sienna follows me into the kitchen, but she looks reluctant. "I'm not sure normal sugar works. They used special stuff from a fancy bottle."

"Ah, sure it will," I assert. "Ours will be even better. It'll be *all natural*. Let's try it. Jump up on the counter and lie down; I'll give you a facial first." I lay two folded kitchen dish towels on the counter for Sea's head, and she gets in place.

"Are you sure this is okay? I feel weird up here. What if your mom comes in?"

"She won't mind," I assure her. I walk over to the pantry and swing open the door. "Okay, let's see, let's see." I scan the shelves but don't see any sugar. We must be out. Hmm. I scan them again. "We've got brown sugar. Think that'll work?"

Sienna shrugs. "I dunno. I guess so."

I grab the bag of brown sugar and pour a bunch into a bowl. "I need a liquid now, to make it mushy for application purposes." I open the fridge door and immediately spot the carton of orange juice. Perfect. It has 100 percent vitamin C too. That's got to be good for your skin. I pour a small amount of the juice into the bowl and mix. Soon I have a thick brown paste. "Okay, close your eyes. I'm going to put this on your T-zone."

Sienna complies and I scoop a handful of the sugar onto her face. It drips down the sides and a little bit goes into her right ear.

"Ah!" she screams. "It's cold!" Another dribble makes its way down into the corner of her mouth. "But surprisingly tasty."

I giggle. "Added benefit to the Tori's Super

Spectacular Sugar Scrub." I grab a towel and wipe up the sugar before it hits her hair.

"Okay. Now I want to work on your cheeks. Eggs. We need eggs." I head back to the refrigerator.

Sienna's eyes dart in my direction, but she doesn't move her head. "Eggs? What are you going to do with eggs?" Her voice is bordering on panicky.

"Don't worry. They're great for your face, I swear. They tighten your skin and shrink your pores."

"They do?" she asks.

"Well, sure. Haven't you ever heard of the phrase 'egg on your face'? That's where it came from," I reply.

"Oh. Okay," she relents. "How do you know all of this stuff about facials?"

"I read a lot," I tell her. Which is true, but not in this case. In this case, I'm winging it.

I take out two eggs and walk back to Sea. She's watching me carefully. "How are you going to put those on me?" she inquires.

Hmm. "Scrambled," I announce. I take out another bowl and a whisk and set to scrambling. I add a splash of milk and salt and pepper out of habit. When the eggs are ready, I use the whisk like a paintbrush and paint egg all over Sea's face.

"Are you sure you know what you're doing?" Sienna says.

"Yes, yes. Just hold still." I finish applying the eggs and examine my handiwork. It's getting there, but she needs something else. I've got it! I head back to the fridge for a third time and pull out a big bottle of ketchup.

"Ketchup?" she exclaims.

"Yes, ketchup. I read somewhere that tomatoes are excellent for you."

"I've heard that too, but I thought they meant to eat," she counters.

"What's good for your inside is good for your outside," I return. "Besides, the ketchup will help keep the eggs moist on your face. It's about layering."

"Well, they *are* getting hard," she agrees. "Okay."

I squirt ketchup all over her face and then use my fingers to spread it out. It looks pretty good, I have to admit. But I feel like I need something to really top it off. I swing open the fridge door and scan the contents again until my gaze settles on just the right thing. Pickles. I take out the jar of pickle chips and tell Sienna to close her eyes. I place a big pickle chip on each of her eyes. "There, you're perfect," I declare.

"What are the pickles for?" Sea asks.

"Bags under the eyes," I say.

"I don't have bags under my eyes," she replies.

"My mom says every woman has bags under her eyes," I counter.

"Well, isn't it cucumbers for bags anyway?" she asks.

"Yes, but a pickle is just a seasoned cucumber. Relax."

"Fine, fine," she mutters. "But how long do I have to leave this stuff on for?"

"Till it dries," I answer. We're both silent for the next minute, listening to the clock tick. "Sea?" I finally say.

"Yeah?"

"You smell like Easter."

"What do you mean I smell like Easter?"

"You know, in a good way. Like in a baked ham–ish sorta way."

"All right, we're taking this stuff off," she insists, trying to sit up.

"No." I put an arm out to stop her and let a tiny giggle escape. She really does look pretty funny. "Just a few minutes more."

"Can I at least take the pickles off and sit up? I'm hungry again."

I think about this. "Okay." I grab her hands and help pull her up to a seated position.

I take out a container of French onion dip and put it on the counter.

"Are you going to put that on me too?" Sienna asks, eyeing the dip.

"No, we're going to eat this." I take a bag of potato chips out of the pantry, rip it open, and set it next to Sea.

"Thanks." She takes a chip and dips it. She pops it in her mouth and then touches her face with one finger and pulls it back to examine it. "I can't believe I let you do this to me." She giggles.

"Yeah, too bad I don't have a camera!" I start to giggle too.

"I'm really broken up about that, let me tell you," she says. "Hey, remember that time in fourth grade when we gave ourselves elaborate makeup jobs with my markers?"

"Oh, my gosh, yes! That was hysterical. Your lids were completely pink from eyelash to eyebrow and mine were purple. And we had those big red circles on our cheeks. Your mom about had a heart attack."

"I know. She kept saying your mother was going to kill her. She relaxed after we told her it was washable marker though," Sea adds.

We continue laughing and eating potato chips. Dad was so right. Everything feels normal again. I have my old Sea back.

I'm feeling very confessional all of a sudden, and I decide I'm going to tell Sea everything—how I completely made Sebastian up because I was hurt from being ignored the last half of the summer and feeling a little jealous and competitive over the new attention she's been getting. And then she'll admit that she made Antonio up as well and we'll have a good laugh over how silly we both were. I open my mouth to speak.

"Man, could you imagine if Antonio saw me like this?" Sea asks. "Talk about testing your love—"

"Oh, stop it already, Sea, geez," I blurt out, completely irked that she ruined the moment with her incessant Antonio talk.

Sienna stops eating chips and gives me a startled look. "Stop what?"

All of this ridiculous made-up boyfriend bragging, I want to say. But I can't get the words out. So I stall instead. "Er, um, double-dipping your chips," I say, and pull the chip dip away from her.

"Sea? Sea?" I pause, listening for her breathing. "Are you asleep?" The room is dark and Sea and I are in our sleeping bags lying on the floor in my bedroom, head to head. I was talking about visiting my dad last weekend as a kind of lead-in to the Talk. I thought we could have a heart-to-heart about this fake boyfriend stuff now that we've had this nice familiar night and it's dark and she can't see my face and I can't see hers to know if she's mad or what. And if either of us cries, the other won't know. But now she went and fell asleep. Well. She knows the rules of First to Sleep. Of course, we didn't *say* we were playing First to Sleep tonight, but it's been a pretty typical thing at our sleepovers so Sea should know better.

I sit up on my knees and begin to rummage through Sienna's backpack, looking for something to freeze. Perfect! Socks. Sea's no stranger to going home in a frozen bra or not being able to brush her teeth in the morning because her toothpaste is a brick. And I've had my share of frozen T-shirts. But neither of us has done socks before. I quietly slip out of the room and head for the kitchen. I fling open the freezer door and toss Sienna's balled up socks toward the back. I grab a lone cookie off a plate on the table on my way out and head back to my room.

My alarm clock says it's 11:34. Way too early for any good sleepover to shut down. I can't believe Sea fell asleep on me like that. She must be really wiped out from all of her storytelling.

Might as well go online. I launch my instant messenger for a quick peek to see if any of my friends are on. Dad!

TorItUp: What are you doing online at this hour?

jbarnes: Hey! That's my line.

TorItUp: ☺ Sienna's sleeping over and she already conked out. I'm bored.

jbarnes: Would your mother let you on this late? Don't respond to any messages from strangers.

TorItUp: You neither! ☺

jbarnes: Did you two clear things up?

TorItUp: Not exactly.

jbarnes: ???

TorItUp: Well, we had fun and everything. I guess things aren't familiar enough for her though because she's still lying.

jbarnes: Hmm. I vote for getting things out in the open. Tell her how you're feeling over breakfast tomorrow. But wait until her mouth is full to talk to her about it. That way if she feels ambushed she can think about what she wants to say while she's chewing.

TorItUp: Interesting technique. I may use it the next time you ask me what grade I got on my math test.

jbarnes: ☺ All right, dearest. Now sign off

and straight to bed. Remember, no

talking to weirdos on the Internet.

TorItUp: But I'm talking to you . . .

jbarnes: ☺ Love you!

TorItUp: Love you back!

I smile to myself and sign off IM per Dad's request. He's so cute when he parents via telecommuting.

13

Pluck my feathers and stick a plastic timer in my butt because I'm a C-H-I-C-K-E-N.

I had the best of intentions to take Dad's advice and talk to Sienna over breakfast this morning. Really, I did. There we were at the kitchen table, a box of Fruity Pebbles between us, and I couldn't bring myself to do it. It felt so confrontational, and I hate confrontation. And besides, why should *I* be doing all the work? She should be remembering old times and feeling like things are *normal* with us after our sleepover and come clean, right? She's the one who lied first.

No, my best friend is some kind of compulsive liar. That's all there is to it. She can't help herself. Maybe she doesn't even know she's doing it. Maybe she's delusional. She obviously needs help and nobody sees it but me. The sleepover wasn't enough to get Sienna to stop the lying. I'm not sure what is. She said she was going to IM Antonio as soon as she got home today.

It's Saturday afternoon, and Sienna's mom picked her up from my house over an hour ago. Something needs to happen soon, and I'm not aware of any twelve-step programs for girls with fake boyfriends. Sea and I have been best friends since kindergarten, so if anyone is going to get her to kick the lying habit, it's going to have to be me. Like that time with the maple tree—I'm going up to get her.

I make sure Mom is busy and not going to bother me for a while. I shut my bedroom door and launch a Web browser. My home page, Google, pops up, and I type in the search phrase "why best friends lie." There are about fifty million hits. Apparently I'm not the first person to have a best friend with a lying problem.

I click on link after link after link. It's amazing the things people lie about. A lot of it seems to be people making themselves sound better than they are. Like this on the Dear Tara advice site:

Dear Tara,

My friends and I don't know what to do. We have this other "friend" who we think is a complete liar. She says that the Jonas Brothers are her cousins yet she can't get us tickets to any of their concerts. She says she has this great big ginormous house with a huge pool, monster TV, and a Wii with every game ever released in the American market yet she can't have people over to visit. Now she says she's going to be in the next Kate Hudson movie and it will be filming this summer on a beautiful beach on the French Riviera and her parents are flying her there after school lets out. What do you want to bet it will be rated R so we can't see it? We tell her that we know she's lying but she insists that she's telling the truth. It's so annoying! What should we do?

Signed,

Annoyed in Denver, CO

And Tara's response:

Dear Annoyed,

Wow, I can see how frustrating this is for you guys. It sounds like your "friend" really wants you to like her. You must be a great group of kids to hang around. Maybe you should cut this "friend" a bit of a break. It sounds like she's feeling inferior around you

guys and she's making things up to get you to
like her. Would you like her if she wasn't really a
cousin of the Jonas Brothers? And she didn't
have the pool or the Wii? No movie to shoot in
the summer? If the answer is yes, then let her
know that you like her for who she is. If she
feels like who she is *is* okay, then she'll stop
trying to be somebody else.

—Tara

Huh. Interesting. I can see Tara's point in this situation, but I'm not sure that it applies to Sea and me. She sure doesn't feel inferior to me; we've been best friends for way too long for something like that to pop up now. And she's not making *lots* of stuff up. She's just making up one specific person. Her "boyfriend." But I won't completely rule it out. I'm going to take all advice into consideration.

I read for the next two hours, taking notes and trying to absorb absolutely everything I can about liars. It's scary how many people have this problem. There are families that break up over lies and people who can't keep jobs because no one can trust them. It seems like once liars get comfortable lying they do it forever. Well, I can't let that happen to Sea. I need to save her now before she embraces this lying life too tightly and there's no turning back.

I compile my research into a plan of attack, and I'm hopeful that it's going to work. Operation Save Sea From Herself (OSSFH) starts Monday.

SSFH, a list:

1. Let her know that who she is *is* okay.
2. Make her feel safe.
3. Try to relate to her situation.
4. Help her to avoid situations in which she tends to lie.
5. Encourage her when she tells the truth.

I walk into school Monday morning with my list on a folded sheet of notebook paper, tucked down in the back pocket of my jeans. I'm feeling really good about the work I've done and ready to tackle this problem head-on. Sienna is at her locker, talking to Lauren and Anica and gathering her stuff for first period. The first item on my Save Sea list keeps flashing in my head. Who you are is okay. Who you are is *okay*.

"Sea!" I say brightly.

"Hey, Tori," Sea replies. "I was just telling Lauren

and Anica about the facial you gave me on Friday night."

"Yeah, I can't believe you put ketchup on her face," Lauren says, making an ick face.

I shrug. "It seemed like a good idea. Though Sienna sure doesn't need facials anyway. Her skin is so naturally radiant all the time, don't you think?"

Lauren looks at Sea's face and then back to me and shrugs. "I guess."

"Wow. Thanks, Tori." Sea giggles nervously.

"Don't thank me. It's your skin. It's almost as glowing as your personality. Which is really super by the way. You're so nice and fun and great to be around. A really fantastic person." I pat Sea on the shoulder.

She raises her eyebrows in this slightly horrified way. Like how someone might look if their mom picked them up from school sporting hair rollers. That happened to me once in the fourth grade. I shudder even thinking about it.

Lauren and Anica shift uncomfortably.

"Um, well, we'll see you guys later," Anica says.

"Yeah, bye," Lauren adds, and the two walk quickly down the hall.

"What's with you?" Sienna asks, once the girls are out of earshot.

"I don't know what you mean," I counter.

"You're acting kind of weird," she says. "That stuff you said was totally embarrassing in front of Lauren and Anica."

"It was? I'm sorry, I didn't mean it to be." I was only trying to let her know that she was okay.

Sienna frowns. "Hmm. Well, all right then. Let's get to homeroom before we're late."

We arrive in homeroom seconds before the bell rings and slide into our seats. Natalie and Avery are already in their seats, talking about their horrible morning bus ride. It seems the bus driver had to pull over three times to talk to some rowdy sixth graders.

We listen for a minute, and then Avery turns to Sienna. "So, how was your weekend? More late-night IMing with Antonio?" she asks, singing Antonio's name.

Sea grins. "Oh yeah. We IMed so late last night that I actually fell asleep on my laptop. The last thing I sent was 't6y6ht6y.'" The girls laugh.

I slip the paper with the OSSFH list out of my pocket and eye number two. Make her feel safe.

"Hey, Sea," I say.

She turns her head toward me. "Yeah?"

I keep my voice low so Avery and Natalie can't hear me. "You know that you can tell me anything, absolutely anything, and I promise I won't get angry. I'll always be your friend no matter what." I take a deep breath. "Is there anything you want to tell me?"

Sienna gives me the crazy eye. "No thanks, Dr. Phil." She looks a little irritated. "Sheesh, what's your deal today, Tori? Stop being such a weirdo." She turns around to face Avery and Natalie.

"No deal," I say to her back. "I just want you to feel safe . . ." Oh, man. I'm not supposed to *tell* her what I'm doing! "I mean, uh, nothing. I didn't mean anything. Go on with your story."

Okay, I'm going to have to be a lot more careful or this isn't going to work. If she knows what I'm doing, she'll get mad and I won't help her at all.

In the hallway between third and fourth period, I spot Sea at the water fountain getting a drink. I figure it's as good a time as any to try to relate to her (number three on the list). I race over to her side as she's wiping some water off her chin.

"Hey, what's up?" I say, leaning against the wall.

Sienna straightens and narrows her eyes at me, like she's trying to figure out what I'm up to. "Nothing. Getting a drink."

"I love your shoes."

Sienna looks down at her black ankle boots. "You do? Gee, thanks."

I nod. "Actually, they make me think of this one time when I was ten and there were these beautiful sparkly ballet flats that I wanted; I *had* to have them. My mom said that I already had a pair of nice dress shoes and didn't need another. I hid the left shoe of my pair in the garage on the morning of a fancy party we were going to and told my mom I couldn't find it so that she'd have to buy me new shoes, and it worked. We had to stop at the shoe store on the way to the party and I got my sparkly flats."

I clear my throat and lean in a little closer. "So," I go on, "did you ever do something like that? You know, tell a lie to get something that you wanted?"

Sienna stares at me for at least twenty seconds, mouth hanging open. Then, in a really slow and condescending voice she says, "If you are done tripping down memory lane, I have an English class to get to."

So much for relating to her.

After history class I head for the cafeteria to grab some lunch and to put the last number on my list, number five (encouragement whenever Sea *does* tell the truth), into action. It's not that I skipped over number four. I tried helping her avoid the situations that she tended to lie in *the entire* morning. But that was just about everything, let me tell you. The only times she didn't tell Antonio stories were when she was in the bathroom or the library (we're not allowed to talk in the library). I had to fake stomach troubles to get her to come with me to the bathroom so many times this morning. And I tried to get her to meet me in the library during study hall, but she refused. She suggested I go lie down in the nurse's office instead.

I get in the lunch line behind Sienna, completely motivated to encourage her so darn much that she'll never lie again. "Hi, Sea," I say cheerfully.

She glances over her shoulder at me. "Oh. Hi," she says flatly.

This isn't a normal Sea response to me, but I've kind of put her through the truth-inducing ringer today. I don't think she knows that I'm trying to help her stop her compulsive lying, but she can tell I'm up to something. I'll have to be sneakier, that's all.

"Was this tuna packed in oil or water?" Sienna asks the lunch lady.

"What's it matter?" the lunch lady slings back.

Sea scoffs. "It matters quite a bit actually. The tuna packed in oil has extra fat."

"She's right," I pipe in with my sparkly positive reinforcement.

Sienna nods at me, appreciating my backing her up.

Pssh. This is so easy.

The lunch lady sighs. "Sweetie, take your lunch and move it along, okay?"

"I will," Sienna says in a huff. She pointedly steps past the tuna and picks up a plain salad.

We pay for our lunches and head for the table. "Could you believe that?" Sienna asks me.

I hesitate. Could *I* believe it? Do I say yes, I believe that it happened, or no, I can't believe it happened? Though it did. I was just there. Oh boy, I'm confused. I smile as encouragingly as I can for my answer.

Sienna sits down at the table, and I take the empty seat next to her.

"I have a completely obscene amount of math homework to do tonight," Natalie moans.

"Tell me about it," Sea says. "I have an insane amount of homework tonight too."

I nod. "That's right! You do."

Sienna cocks her head and gives me a look. I shove my apple into my mouth so I don't have to say anything.

Yum. Fuji.

"Well, I have to get all A's this quarter to fund my winter wardrobe," Natalie says.

I raise my eyebrows, and Avery explains. "Her mom pays her for each A."

"Oh," I say. Wish my mom and dad paid me for A's.

"I bought this outfit over the weekend," Natalie says. She looks down at her clothes.

"I was going to mention it," Sienna says. "Your skirt is so cute. I have one in blue."

I clap my hands and yell out, "Yes, you do, Sea! Good one!"

No one says a word. Sienna isn't the only one giving me the crazy eye now. The whole table is looking at me. Maybe my truth cheerleading is a bit too much. It seemed to be working at first. I think I need to tone down my enthusiasm a little and not be so vocal about reinforcing her good behavior.

I turn around like I need to check the clock on the wall. Really I'm hoping that when I turn back around the conversation will have moved on to something else.

It works and the girls switch topics and I try to do more listening than talking. I busy myself unwrapping my giant chocolate chip cookie.

"My mom grounded me from the Internet for the day," Avery says, "because I didn't have time to clean up my room last night. I mean, it's my room anyway. I don't know why she is so harsh."

"My mom gets like that too," Sienna says.

That's true. I break off a tiny piece of my cookie and slide it over to Sea. She pops it in her mouth.

"I can't leave for school without my bed being made every morning," Sienna continues.

I've heard her say this before. I slide another piece of cookie over to Sea, and she picks it up and eats it.

"And if I leave a wet towel in my room for even five minutes, the woman explodes," Sea says.

Oh yeah. I've seen Mrs. Baker turn purple over a wet towel on the floor. I push a third piece of cookie at Sea, and she eats it without even looking at it.

"To keep the peace I just do a five-minute quick clean of my room every night. It's worth it to avoid the fight if I don't," Sienna concludes.

Yeah. She's been doing the five-minute cleanup thing for years. I slide another piece of cookie toward her.

She whirls around to face me, anger in her eyes.

Uh-oh.

"What are you doing?" she snarls at me.

I try to giggle. "What do you mean?"

"The cookies," she says. "What's the deal with the cookies? Are you rewarding me with treats like a dog or something?"

I feel the blood drain from my face. Busted. "Gosh no," I say, "I would never give a dog chocolate."

Yeah. Not the totally right thing to say.

Sienna jumps to her feet, slapping her hands on the table. "Tori, I've had it! Until you start behaving like a normal person again, don't talk to me!" With that, she turns and stomps off.

Well, that was a big ol' bust. Positive reinforcement? Not so positive.

To be honest, I guess my list sort of sucked. I don't know why I thought any of these things would work. There'll be no Tori's Truth-Telling Tips seminars for me to teach anywhere in the near future, that's for sure.

But I can't give up. I'm down but I'm so not out. There is one more thing I can do. I really didn't want to do this though. It's a total last resort. It didn't even make my list, that's how last resort it is.

I have to hypnotize her.

15

There's this thing I stumbled upon online when I was doing my research the other day—it's called covert hypnosis. Supposedly it's a way that you can secretly hypnotize another person and get them to do what you want without them ever knowing. How amazing is that? You would think people everywhere would be capitalizing on this. According to the Web site, I have to have a good rapport with her (easy since we're best friends), then I have to captivate her attention (I can be captivating when I want to be), and make some suggestions (or in this case, one specific suggestion: Stop lying, Sea!). We'll see if it works.

The final school bell rings and I race to get to Sienna's locker before she does. I see her coming, and when she notices me she stops and looks around. She's probably trying to find a way out without talking to me, but I'm not budging and I know she needs her things. Sea realizes this too and slowly trudges toward me. Before she can say a word I say, "Sea, I'm really *really* sorry about how goofy I was acting today. I don't know what got into me, but it was a really weird day. I think maybe I was just thrown off, you know? I got in this horrible fight with my mom this morning and it has made the whole day a mess." Sea and her mom fight a lot, so I know this will get her.

Sienna pops open her locker and begins to load her backpack with books and notebooks. "Oh, I know how that is. Don't worry about it, Tori. I'm over it," she replies. She finishes gathering her stuff and zips her bag closed.

"Really?" Wow. I completely expected begging to be involved. I'm getting off easy. "Thanks, Sea. You're such a great friend."

"No prob. I'd better get going. My mom is waiting outside." She turns to go, but I reach out a hand to stop her.

"Your mom is so nice picking you up from school every day. I wish mine would. But she's always too busy for me." I try to look sad. "I hate going home to an empty house," I add.

Sienna shifts from one leg to another. "Um, well, do you want to come over for a while or something?"

"Could I? That would be great!" Omigod, omigod,

omigod! This stuff actually works. I totally just made her invite me over. This is *so* freakin' cool.

"Yeah, let's go," she says, and I follow her out to her car.

Ten minutes later we're standing in front of Sienna's new tan leather couch in her family room. I haven't been over to her house since she got back from vacation, and it looks fantastic. Her mom has been busily remodeling everything. There is this sort of beachy spa resort vibe going on—lots of marble and rock sculptures with water dribbling down them, big palm trees and wicker baskets and bamboo tables strategically placed about. And, if I'm not mistaken, there is one of those soothing ocean sounds CDs being piped through some kind of surround sound speaker system. That, or I'm losing my mind, because I swear I just heard a seagull overhead.

"Mrs. Baker, everything looks so beautiful," I say. Sea rolls her eyes, but her mom's face lights up.

"Really?" She puts her hands on her hips and surveys the room like she's looking at it for the first time. I can tell she's pleased with her work. "It's coming along. At least I got rid of that old couch, huh?"

She's talking about the plaid pullout sofa bed they had forever. I think Sienna's dad even had it in college.

It was definitely worn in but it still had charm if you ask me. Sea and I had countless sleepovers on that old thing. It held great memories. Last winter during one of our sleepovers we were messing around with the bed—jumping on the head of the pullout bed so the foot flew up in the air. I jumped a little too hard one time and fell down in between the sofa cushions and the bed. It didn't hurt and actually turned out in a happy ending. I found my Strawberry Shortcake doll I had lost when I was seven while stuck down there. I'd always thought Mom got rid of it in a donation pile or something, but nope, it was sitting under Sea's couch for five years. I probably should have asked Mrs. Baker to look through the couch before ditching it to see if I'd lost anything else.

"Would you girls like some fresh-baked cookies?" Mrs. Baker asks.

I nod vigorously and Sea rolls her eyes again.

"Be right back," her mom calls, walking out of the room.

"She didn't freshly bake anything," Sea mutters after her mom is out of earshot. "All she does is shop."

"You say that like it's a bad thing," I return.

Sienna shrugs. "I just don't see why she's pretending to bake when she probably bought them from some fancy bakery."

"Homemade, store-made, it doesn't matter to me. They're all little circles of bliss in my belly." I pat my stomach.

Sea smiles. Because she knows it's true.

I study Sea's face and though she looks like she's okay, I can still see irritation in her eyes. It's interesting that she gets this upset with her mom for pretending when she's doing the exact same thing.

"Want to play Wii or something?" Sea asks, perched on the arm of the couch.

"Yeah, sounds fun." I take a seat on one end of the couch and my back end feels like it died and went to heaven, that's how soft and ridiculously comfortable the couch is. I close my eyes for a moment, enjoying the cushiony goodness, and I'm startled when Sea tosses the Wii remote in my lap.

She pops in a Star Wars game and we choose our characters. Yoda for her, Obi-Wan Kenobi for me. I've always admired Obi-Wan's lightsaber skills. And he's still the only guy I've ever seen who can pull off a braided tail.

"Remember when we first saw Star Wars—the one with Hayden Christensen as Anakin?" I ask. It was one of our first times in a real movie theater. Dad was still living at home with Mom and me. The theater was almost empty, and he let us sit two rows ahead of him so that we could pretend like we were grownups.

Sea smiles. "Yeah." She starts our game.

"He was so cute and we both had huge crushes on him. We used to talk about what it would be like to date him," I add. Sea even ripped a picture of him out of a teen magazine and hung it on the wall in her room. She used to kiss him good night every night.

"I remember. He was always so good to that Queen Amidala. He loved her so much." Sienna sighs. She has always referred to her as "that Queen Amidala." Like she wasn't good enough for Hayden Christensen or something.

"Yeah. And we used to say we needed to find a guy like that. A guy who *really* loved us. Remember?" I ask.

"Uh-huh," Sea replies, moving her small Yoda character through the desert, looking for clones.

She seems pretty agreeable so far. I might as well go for it.

"You can have a *real* guy who *really* loves you, Sea," I say. I make my Obi-Wan Kenobi cut off two Sand People's heads and hop into his Jedi ship.

"Uh-huh."

It's working.

"You can have a *real* boyfriend," I say. I'm pretty proud of myself for how quickly I've mastered this whole covert hypnotism thing.

"Yeah," she mumbles.

GAME PAUSE.

Sea turns to me. "Okay, wait. What the heck are you saying?"

Whoops. She looks kind of mad.

"What?" I hope my innocent face is coming across. Though any face other than my guilty one will do.

"What is all this real boyfriend stuff? What are you trying to say?"

Oh, yikes. Not good. Like her Yoda character, *the force in her, strong it is.* "Huh?" I offer. "I don't know. I thought we were talking about Star Wars. What are you talking about?"

Sea hesitates and furrows her eyebrows. She looks confused. "I'm not sure," she replies slowly. "Never mind. Let's play." She turns back to the television and unpauses the game.

Phew. That could have been so ugly. I'm never going to try to hypnotize anyone ever again.

16

Sometimes a good night's sleep makes everything seem different in the morning. Yesterday I was desperate to save Sienna from her compulsive lying self. But today things have changed somehow. So, my best friend is a little colorful. So, she's minorly loose with the truth. Some might call it charming. Even creative. And what's it hurting anyway? There's no damage being done here. If anything, things are better for both of us. The only repercussions from our abundance of lying are that our social lives have expanded. Boo hoo hoo. We have more friends. Isn't that what every girl my age wants? Actually, I didn't think I wanted that; I was pretty happy with it being just Sea and me. But it appears that lots of friends *is* what the average girl wants. And here I am trying to ruin it. Pssh. No more. In fact, I'm going to embrace my fake boyfriend (not literally of course) and really live it up. We're going to have the most fantastic fake relationship *ever*. Even if our new friends aren't *friend* friends, who cares? It's all about perception anyway, and right now I'm perceived to have an awesome boyfriend and a popular best friend. There is nothing wrong with that.

I carefully pick out my clothes, deciding on a light pink cable-knit elbow sweater and brown skirt. I reach up into my closet for the small wooden jewelry box tucked in the corner to the far right. Inside are a few pieces of jewelry I've received over the years from Mom and Grandma and my aunt Kate. There is a birthstone ring, a chunky silver bracelet, and several pairs of earrings. I zone in on one particular item though: a small blue Tiffany box. Inside lies a silver open heart pendant with a pink sapphire at the top of it. Sienna's never seen it and I've never told her about it. I haven't told anyone about it. I haven't worn it anywhere because it's so expensive. I call it Dad's guilt gift (only in my head and not to Dad, of course). I also never wear it because Mom was way royally ticked when Dad gave it to me. I remember her yelling things like "Are you out of your mind? Tiffany for a nine-year-old? You never gave me anything Tiffany." I figured it would make her angry so I put it away up on my closet shelf and forgot about it. Until now, that is.

"Ready to go, Tori?" Mom yells.

"Yeah. I'm coming," I respond. I tuck the heart underneath my sweater—I still don't see any reason to tick Mom off—grab my backpack, and head out the front door.

I open the passenger door of the car and climb in.

"Oh, honey, you look so nice. Something special going on today?" Mom asks.

"Nope. Just felt like dressing up," I reply.

She backs the car down the driveway and into the street. "How are things going at school? I'm really sorry that I've been so preoccupied at work. I've been working on this big project for one of our top clients, and Linda, that no-good suck-up, has been trying to edge me out of my lead position and . . ."

I tune her out. Now that she's ranting, it'll probably last the whole way to school. The good thing is that she never expects me to respond, so I can daydream or think about my own problems. Which, if you ask me, are a lot more complicated than hers.

We pull up to the junior high, and I wave goodbye to Mom. We got here early today and kids are still milling around outside. I zero in on Sienna, Lauren, Anica, Avery, and Natalie talking by the bike rack. I pull the heart pendant out from beneath my sweater and smooth it down so that it's in clear view.

"Morning," I call cheerily as I join the group.

"Hey, Tori." Sienna smiles. "We were talking about *Brooks Prep*. Did you see the new episode last night?"

I finger my heart pendant. "No, I was sort of busy last night."

"Oh, it was awesome!" Sea exclaims. "Darcy broke up with Jacob and—"

"Wait," Lauren interrupts, putting up a hand to shush Sienna. "Is that Tiffany?"

She points to my necklace and I blush. I didn't even have to try to blush—it just happened. I nod.

"No. Way," Sienna utters.

"I knew it." Lauren claps her hands. "My mom gets the Tiffany catalogs and I've been studying them for years. I can always spot a Tiffany. It's really pretty, Tori."

"Thank you," I reply.

"Where'd you get it?" Sea asks.

A huge grin spreads across my face. "I was coming over to tell you. It's from Sebastian. We're exclusive now."

"Oh," Avery gasps, clutching her heart.

"That's so sweet," Natalie coos.

"Exclusive? So what does that mean?" Sienna asks.

"It means they're getting married," Avery cries.

"No, that's engaged," Anica says.

"Yeah, she's right," I affirm. "We're not engaged. Not yet, anyway. We could be though. Someday. Being exclusive is like the step before getting engaged." *And then we'll have a fake wedding and a fake house and three adorable fake children. But no fake cats. I'm allergic.*

The girls look impressed. Sienna looks upset. My guess is she's racking her brain trying to figure out a way for Antonio to top this, and unless he sends a unicorn to whisk her off to Aruba for a rendezvous, he can't.

"I don't get . . . When did this happen?" Sea mumbles. "You were at my house yesterday afternoon."

"It was after. When my mom and I pulled up to our house, Sebastian was sitting there on the porch steps waiting for me. His mom was in the area for some kind of meeting and dropped him off to visit for a while. He gave it to me then." You know, this lying thing gets easier the more you do it.

"He also gave me a poem," I continue. "A love poem. It was about stars and eyes and hearts beating. It was so romantic."

"He wrote it?" Sea asks hesitantly.

I consider saying yes and adding poet to his list of amazing qualities, but she already looks crushed enough about this latest development. "Nah, I think it was by some old dead guy. It was really good though."

The warning bell rings. "Let's go in." I walk toward the main doors and the girls are following *me.* Sea poutily brings up the rear.

Sienna is moody for the rest of the day. She's barely said two words about Antonio. It's like she's defeated or something. My Sebastian is the crown prince of fake boyfriends and her Antonio is but a mere imitation. Literally, ha ha. She's not even trying to compete, even when the opportunity is handed right to her. Like at lunch today I was telling the girls how Sebastian told me he was going to ask his mom if they could invite me on their family vacation this summer to Lake Geneva. It was the perfect opportunity for Sienna to dredge up yet another one of her vacation stories about Antonio. But did she? Nope. She just sat there stabbing her fat-free pudding cup over and over again with her spork.

And when the final bell rang and we were getting our books and things ready to go, I said how I couldn't wait to get home and see if Sebastian had e-mailed me anything cute. I came right out and asked her if she was going to IM with Antonio tonight and she just shrugged. That was it. She's really being a big baby today if you ask me. She reminds me of my little cousin Lily. If you're playing Monopoly with her and she's ahead, then everything is great. But soon as someone else starts winning she up and quits.

* * *

Later that evening, while Mom's making dinner in the kitchen—mostaccioli and turkey meatballs—I check my e-mail and halfway expect to see an e-mail from Sebastian. I've been making up so many stories about him that he almost seems real. I see an e-mail from Dad and click on it.

> **To:** TorItUp@funmail.com
> **From:** jbarnes@zmail.com
> **Re:** Dearest Daughter
>
> Dear Tori,
>   How are you? How's school going this week? I can't wait for your next visit—I'm thinking we'll hit Navy Pier next time. What do you think? Did you and Sienna get everything straightened out?
> I love and miss you,
> Dad

I pull my heart pendant from underneath my sweater and rub it. I hit Reply.

> **To:** jbarnes@zmail.com
> **From:** TorItUp@funmail.com
> **Re:** Dearest Father

Dear Dad,

I love and miss you too! I think Navy
Pier the next time I visit is an excellent
idea. I ♥ the Ferris wheel. School is fine and
everything is going well with me and
Sienna. I'm actually having fun. I decided it
was too hard to get her to change so I
joined her. My fake boyfriend is kicking her
fake boyfriend's butt!
I love you,
Tori

I minimize my e-mail and head to the kitchen for dinner with Mom. When I'm full I retreat back to my room for "homework" and check my e-mail again. Two new e-mails. One from Sienna and one from Dad.

To: ToritUp@funmail.com
From: SiennasHeart@funmail.com
Re: Math

What was tonight's homework?

That's it. A one-line e-mail. Sheesh, somebody's in a mood. I hit Reply.

To: SiennasHeart@funmail.com

From: TorItUp@funmail.com

Re: Re: Math

P34, 1–21, odds

There. I can write short e-mails too. I open the
e-mail from Dad.

To: TorItUp@funmail.com

From: jbarnes@zmail.com

Re: Dearest Truthful Integrity-Filled Daughter

Dear Tori,

No, no, no. You're missing the point,
hon. Don't be someone you're not. You
don't need a fake boyfriend to be special
and you don't need to compete with your
best friend. Just be you. You are perfect.
Love always,
Dad

Competing? We're not competing. Okay, yeah we
are. But I'm winning, so there's no harm. I hit Reply.

To: jbarnes@zmail.com

From: TorItUp@funmail.com

Re: Dearest Worrying Needlessly Father

Dear Dad,

    You needn't worry as I am very wise and capable far beyond my twelve years. Besides I'd think you'd prefer me dating an imaginary boy as opposed to a real one, no?

I love you,

Tori

There. Send. I have everything under control.

17

I head into school Wednesday morning, ready for whatever Antonio the Great stories Sienna has to throw at me. I figure she spent most of last night coming up with something *big* to beat out Sebastian's generous jewelry gift yesterday. I know that's what I was doing, preparing my counterattack to her counterattack. But she did nothing. She didn't have one Antonio story to tell in homeroom this morning. Instead she pretended to be overly interested in Channel One and the story about the ninth-grade girl from the inner city who was chosen to spend two weeks in Africa this summer distributing aid to the poor. Avery and Natalie still wanted to chat, of course, so I did my best to keep them entertained with tales of Sebastian's and my relationship.

After homeroom, I practically bounce into science class.

"Hi!" I say, slipping into my seat next to Daphne.

"Tori!" Daphne and Bella squeal.

"Are you ready?" Daphne inquires.

"So ready," I return. "Did you talk to your brother, Bella? Is everything on schedule on his end?"

"Yes!" she exclaims, rapping her fists on her desk. We're all super pumped about our plan. It's hard to sit still. "He said the cat lady—I mean Principal Brown—dropped off her film for developing last night. She always picks it up on Wednesday afternoons, so it's now or never."

Principal Brown, a.k.a. "the cat lady," is an amateur photographer with only one subject in her presumably huge portfolio. Mrs. Winifred Whiskers. According to Bella's older brother, Christian, Principal Brown takes thirty new pictures of her cat in various cute outfits each week and *always* brings them to the photo lab where he works on Tuesdays for pickup on Wednesday afternoons. He said if we want to slip something into her photos, we have to e-mail it to him by noon today. Our plan is to tell a story with pictures. It's a story we're thinking Principal Brown will find *very* interesting.

Daphne is clutching her phone in her hand.

"Did you already get the picture of the door with the room number?" I question.

"Yeah," Daphne replies. "I got it on the way in."

"I'm up then," Bella announces. "Can you help me?

Distract Mrs. Wittler while she's drinking from her cup so she doesn't see me take the pic."

"No problem," I say. We look at Mrs. Wittler, sitting in the front with her coffee cup in one hand and the attendance sheet in the other. I walk toward her.

"Yes, Tori?" she says, setting her attendance sheet down on the table and wrapping both hands around the cup.

"Um, Mrs. Wittler?" I begin.

She nods and takes a sip from her cup, keeping her eyes on me.

"Do we have a quiz today?"

She sets her cup down and frowns. "Tori, go sit down. I'll tell the entire class what we're doing at the same time."

"Oh. Okay. Thanks," I say, and return to my seat. "Did you get it?" I whisper to Bella.

Bella nods and mouths, "You're up."

Class starts and Mrs. Wittler tells us to write a one-paragraph reaction to yesterday's experiment. The room is quiet. I slip Daphne's phone into my pocket since it's my turn to take a picture. I raise my hand and ask if I can use the girls' bathroom, and Mrs. Wittler nods.

I leave class but I never go to the bathroom. Instead I stand in the hallway, peeking in at Mrs. Wittler sitting at her lab table. She's clutching her cup of coffee while she watches the room. Everyone is working. I see her look down at her large cloth bag on the floor and then back at the students. And then back at the bag again. This is it.

Mrs. Wittler slowly reaches down to her bag and pulls out the flask, hiding it under the table. She scans the room of working students once more, probably trying to see if anyone is paying any attention to her, screws off the top of the flask, and pours some of the liquid into her cup.

Snap! I've got the picture.

I wait out in the hallway for another minute before reentering the class. I give Daphne and Bella a thumbs-up and slide into my seat.

Daphne is going to take the last two photos, so I pass her the phone when I'm sure no one is looking. I start working on my paragraph.

Maybe two minutes later, Daphne stands and approaches Mrs. Wittler. I can't hear what she's saying, but I know what the plan is. She's going to tell Mrs. Wittler that her pen ran out of ink and ask to borrow one. Mrs. Wittler keeps her extra pens in the top drawer of her desk in her office. Mrs. Wittler waves for her to go ahead, and Daphne walks slowly down the aisle between Bella and me. We see her quietly flip open the phone and take a picture of Mrs. Wittler's office. I glance around the room to see if anyone noticed, but the entire class is busily working. Except for us, that is.

Daphne enters Mrs. Wittler's office and a few moments later rejoins us with a new pen in hand.

I watch the front of the room. Mrs. Wittler is looking down at the table, reading something. I lean over to Daphne. "Did you get a pic of the whiskey?" I ask. She nods.

Yes!

After class we meet in the girls' bathroom and e-mail the pictures to Christian in the order they are to be printed—Wittler's room number, Wittler drinking from her cup, Wittler pouring from her flask into the cup, Wittler's office, and Wittler's whiskey lying in her desk.

Man, I wish I could see Principal Brown's face when she picks up her photos today.

18

I make it into homeroom on Thursday right before the bell rings. Sienna and the girls are already talking up a storm. She's noticeably more chipper today. Good. I'm glad. Maybe a couple of days of feeling defeated is what she needed and now she'll go back to normal. Sea looks up at me as I approach.

"What's everyone talking about?" I ask, slipping into my desk chair.

"There is a new substitute teacher in science," Natalie answers. "Mrs. Wittler is gone. I heard she got busted for selling drugs out of the trunk of her car." She nods, her eyes wide.

"I heard she embezzled money from the science club," Sienna asserts.

"I heard she hooked up with one of her former students," Avery counters.

Man, the rumors are flying already. "Ewwww.

That's so gross! I bet it's none of that. Maybe she's on vacation?" I offer. "I'm sure she'll be back."

Sienna shakes her head. "Uh-uh. The sub said she was here until they find a permanent replacement."

"Permanent?" I repeat. Oh wow. I guess our little photo story worked. But why do I suddenly feel bad? I mean, she wasn't exactly ever nice to any of us. And we had no choice but to report her for drinking in class. But I didn't want to ruin her life or anything. I didn't want to get her fired. I figured they'd send her to a fancy rehab for a month like they do with all of the celebrities who can't stop partying. Yikes. I look out the classroom door into the hallway. I wonder if Daphne and Bella have heard yet.

"So hey, the back-to-school dance is Saturday night," Avery states, changing the subject. "Are you going?"

"Huh?" I utter. I'm still thinking about Mrs. Wittler. An image of her homeless on the street, eating bits of chewed-up, thrown-out cheeseburger from a Dumpster is going through my mind. I hope she can find another job. Well, first I hope she can get some help with her drinking and then find a new job.

"The dance," Avery repeats. "Are you going?"

"Oh. I totally forgot about the dance," I reply. "I guess I'll go. If I have time to get a dress, that is. I'll have to talk to my mom."

"It's not formal or anything. You can wear what you want," Natalie says. "We're going. It'll be so much fun. You have to come."

"Okay," I relent. "Yeah, I'll go."

"Are you going to ask Charles?" Avery teases Natalie.

Natalie's cheeks turn a deep red. "Avery! I told you not to tell anyone." She puts her face in her hands.

"Whoops. Sorry," Avery says. "But they don't care." She waves at Sea and me. "They have boyfriends anyway. They're not going to say anything."

"Aw, you like Charles?" Sea asks. "You should ask him to the dance. I bet he says yes."

"Really?" Natalie shakes her head. "I don't think I can. I'd probably hyperventilate trying to get the words out. Maybe he'll ask me?"

"You should ask him," I pipe in. "He might not even know that you like him."

Channel One flips on while we're chatting, and we stop to watch. There is this extraordinarily gorgeous boy smiling down at us from the television screen. He has wavy light brown hair, big emerald green eyes, pink full lips, and an adorable dimple in his left cheek.

"*Wow,*" Avery says. "Will you look at that?"

"Shh," Sienna says. "I want to hear what they're saying."

We stare at the screen. There is a half-burned build-ing and red fire trucks lining a street in the city, their lights flashing. The teenage newscaster continues with the story. "He's only fourteen and in the eighth grade at McHenry Junior High School here in Chicago. The mother of the two toddlers that he rescued from the burning apartment building says she feels like she has another son. She will be eternally grateful to Sebastian Colander, our local hero."

Sienna, Avery, and Natalie audibly gasp and fling around in their chairs to look at me. I almost fall out of mine and clutch the desk to keep myself steady.

Did they just say Sebastian Colander? Like, Sebas-tian Colander, the exact name of my fake boyfriend, Sebastian Colander? What are the freakin' odds of that?

Have I taken a breath lately? I need to keep breath-ing.

I inhale deeply. Ah yes. Air. There it is. Oh. My. God. Sebastian is on television!

"Tori!" Sienna yells. "You said Sebastian was gor-geous, but omigod, he's like celebrity gorgeous."

"He's *amazing*," Natalie adds.

"Holy crap, Tori, he's phenomenal," Avery confirms. "And *you* are exclusive with him. You are the luckiest girl in our entire school!"

I reach for my heart pendant. Oh yeah. Hee hee.

Sebastian gave me this beautiful necklace. Why am I feeling dizzy? I gasp. Right. That breathing thing. Must keep doing that breathing thing.

"Tori, you have to, I mean *have to*, bring Sebastian to the school dance on Saturday," Avery insists. "All the girls will go crazy. You'll be the envy of the entire seventh grade. Forget that, you'll be the envy of Norton Junior High."

"Definitely," Natalie agrees. "He's a local celebrity now—like that girl broadcaster said. Wow, I'm already jealous. Do you think he'll give me an autograph? I mean, if you ask him he'll do it, right?"

Everyone is looking at me. I think they want me to speak. I seem to have forgotten how to do that, however.

"Oh, Tori," Sea says. "They're right. You *have* to bring Sebastian to the dance. We can finally have that double date we talked about. My parents are flying Antonio out to go to the dance with me. It'll be so perfect."

I stare at Sea, my mouth hanging open.

Antonio is real?!

I think my heart just stopped.

19

Let's see. The dance is the day after tomorrow. That's plenty of time for me to hunt down the real Sebastian Colander, make him fall in love with me, and bring him to the dance. Right?

Oh lord. I've got to try.

I find Bella in the hallway before first hour. "Bella," I start, stopping her before she goes into class. "Do me a favor?"

"Sure. What's up?" she responds.

"I sort of need to skip out of science class today. It's a sub anyway, so I'm sure she won't even notice that I'm not here." I look around to see if anyone is listening and decide to lower my voice in case someone is. "If she takes attendance, can you fake a 'here' for me?"

Bella gives me a concerned look. "No problem. Are you sick or something? You look like you've seen a ghost."

I tilt my head. *You could say that,* I think. If seeing

one's fake boyfriend materialize before one's very eyes isn't a bit ghostly, I don't know what is. "I'll be okay," I say instead. "Thank you *so* much for doing this. You're a good friend."

After the bell rings and all of the students are in class, I hang out in the hallway outside the school library. I duck behind a big garbage can waiting for the librarian, Mrs. Cass, to leave for her daily coffee break in the teachers' lounge. Boy, the teachers at this school sure like their coffee.

I quietly sneak into the library and let myself onto one of the computers. I open up my e-mail program, hit Compose, and start writing.

To: jbarnes@zmail.com
From: TorItUp@funmail.com
Re: Dearest Wise Butt-Saving Father

Dad!

Oh, Dad, I messed up. I'm in SO MUCH trouble. You have to help me. You know a lot of people in the city. Ever hear of a Sebastian Colander? He goes to McHenry Junior High and he's in the eighth grade. I told everyone he was my boyfriend (the

fake one I mentioned previously) but it
turns out that HE'S REAL! I have to bring
him to the dance this Saturday night.
Can you help me? I need to find him
ASAP. My entire social life depends on
this. We're talking life or death here, Dad.
HELP ME!
Love,
Tori

I hit Send and check the clock. I've been in here for five minutes. I can probably hang out for another five before Mrs. Cass returns and finds me out. I'm hoping Dad sees my e-mail and writes back immediately. He's a chronic e-mail checker, so the chances are good that he will. He's also a chronic Tweeter. I can imagine what he's writing right now in the "What's happening?" box. Let's hope it is "Devising a clever plan to rescue daughter from schoolwide ostracizing."

The adrenaline is coursing through me, and I can hardly sit still. What if Dad can't help me? What am I going to do? I wasn't kidding when I said this was life or death. Now that Antonio's real, *I'm* the only one with a fake boyfriend. And if I get exposed as the big fat liar that I am, how do I ever live it down? This is one of those things that could follow me throughout not only junior high but high school. I'll be a social leper. Not only will no one want to be friends with me but Sea won't want anything to do with me either. I have to fix this.

I click on my in-box to check for any new e-mail. Score. There's one from Dad.

To: TorItUp@funmail.com

From: jbarnes@zmail.com

Re: Dearest Should-Have-Listened-to-Her-Father Daughter

Tori! Tori, Tori, Tori.

Oh, hon, I'm so sorry. This sounds like quite the mess. Chicago is a big city, my dear. I wish I could tell you that I knew everyone and that I could find this Sebastian kid and bring him to the school dance for you, but I can't. I won't tell you that I told you so (at least I won't tell you again. LOL. I know, not an LOL time. Sorry), but I will give you some advice. Sweetie, you've got to come clean. Tell the truth. The truth sets you free (really smart, wise

people around the world concur). You'll get
through this, Tor.
Love always,
Dad

The truth? That's his recommendation? The truth?
Is he freakin' kidding me? What good is the truth going
to do me now?

I close my e-mail and glance around the library. I
have to get out of here before Mrs. Cass discovers me. I
can't exactly go to science class right now though. I need
time to think. I head for the handicapped stall of the
second-floor girls' bathroom: my thinking spot.

It looks like I'm going to have to track down this
Sebastian Colander all by myself.

I spent two entire class periods in the girls' bathroom
today. It took me that long to get up the nerve to face my
friends again. That was fun, let me tell you. News of
my gorgeous famous boyfriend spread like mono at a
game of Spin the Bottle. Everyone wanted to ask questions; everyone wanted to meet him. *Join the club,* I thought.
Not trusting words to come from my mouth and not
wanting to further incriminate myself, I plastered a

good-size smile on my face and nodded a lot. It got me through the day anyway.

I also needed the bathroom downtime to devise a plan of attack for locating Sebastian Colander. And while I wouldn't say it's foolproof, it's a start at least. I'm going to turn where I always turn when I'm in trouble.

Google.

I know I shouldn't be online when Mom's not home. And I swear I'll reserve a nice chunk of time later for feeling immensely guilty about this rule I'm about to break, but desperate times call for desperate measures and all that.

I close my bedroom door and carefully stack a bunch of books against the inside of the door, in case Mom gets home early. I know the books won't keep her out, but they'll give me enough of a warning to shut down my Web browser and get away from the computer.

I search for "Sebastian Colander," and two pages of hits are displayed. Not bad. I click on the links one at a time, looking for anything that might help me locate Sebastian. It seems to be news story after news story about the fire. I click on a link to an online paper for the city.

14-Year-Old Boy Rescues
Woman and Twin Toddlers

CHICAGO, ILLINOIS—McHenry Junior High School eighth graders Sebastian Colander and Darrell Rogers were walking by an apartment building on the 4700 block on South Tripp Avenue Wednesday evening when they spotted smoke pouring from the building. Rogers called 911 while Colander ran through the building, banging on doors, to make sure that everyone had gotten out. "I heard babies crying," Colander said when he reached apartment 2A. "I had to do something so I busted down the door [of the apartment]." Colander followed the crying to a nursery in the back of the apartment where twin two-year-olds, Johnny and Tyler Jackson, were hysterical in their cribs. "I scooped up the kids in my arms and ran out. I saw a lady sleeping on a couch in the living room and yelled at her to get up and follow me out of the building," Colander added. Thirty-four-year-old Sheila Jackson and her boys made it to the sidewalk uninjured shortly before fire trucks arrived. "I can't believe this young boy saved my family," Ms. Jackson told reporters. "I'll forever be grateful." Chicago firefighters later found that the fire had been started by a tipped-over electric heater. Firefighters also commented that the smoke alarm in the apartment did not have batteries. Ms. Jackson noted that she had taken a heavier dose of her allergy medication than normal that night and that was why she didn't notice the fire.

I sit back in my chair and rub my cheek. Dude. My boyfriend is *hot.* Seriously, I have some amazing taste. He really is a hero.

I continue searching the Web for something that will help me reach Sebastian, but I'm not finding anything that looks useful yet. I was really hoping I'd find an e-mail address for him so I could contact him directly. Not that I have any sort of clue as to what I'd say. The closest thing I found was the McHenry Junior High Web site. All the e-mail addresses for the teachers listed on the page end in @MJHS.edu. Although it's a long shot, I'm thinking maybe if I try a bunch of different combinations to that address one of them will reach him.

To: Sebastian.Colander@MJHS.edu, Sebastian_
Colander@MJHS.edu, SColander@MJHS.
edu, ColanderS@MJHS.edu, SColander1@
MJHS.edu

From: TorItUp@funmail.com

Re: Need to speak with you

If this is the real Sebastian Colander,
you need to write me back right away. It is
extremely urgent. Thank you.
Tori Barnes

Send.

I stare at my e-mail, waiting. Hmm. On second thought, he might just send that e-mail right to junk mail, thinking it's spam. And I don't exactly have the luxury of time to wait around and see. I compose another e-mail.

To: Sebastian.Colander@MJHS.edu, Sebastian_
Colander@MJHS.edu, SColander@MJHS.
edu, ColanderS@MJHS.edu, SColander1@
MJHS.edu

From: TorItUp@funmail.com

Re: Need to speak with you, Part 2

This is not spam. I am not from a small
village in Zimbabwe, I am not a Nigerian
prince, and I don't need to use your bank
account or your social security number or

anything like that. I swear. I'm just a girl in the seventh grade at Norton Junior High School in Norton, IL, and I really need to talk to you. Please write me back. Thank you.

Tori Barnes

Send.

There. That's better than nothing. But not enough by far. I need to keep searching. I return to Google, looking for anything to get me closer to Sebastian *now*.

I scroll down to the bottom of the first page of hits and an IM window pops up.

> **SiennasHeart:** Tori!!

Ah! Is there any chance she can see that I'm Googling Sebastian? I mean, her IM window is *so* close to my search box.

No, I'm being paranoid. Of course she can't see what I'm doing. Unless she installed a camera somewhere in my room. I scan my room, looking for a small camera. Stop it! I'm being silly. She didn't put a camera in my room. I write back.

> **ToriItUp:** Hey, Sea
> **SiennasHeart:** Whatcha doing?

TorItUp: Just homework. You?

SiennasHeart: TV. *Survivor* Season 9,365 I
think. LOL.

TorItUp: LOL.

SiennasHeart: Talking to Sebastian?

TorItUp: Not yet.

SiennasHeart: You're going to ask him if he
can come to the dance Saturday, right?

TorItUp: Of course.

SiennasHeart: Good. I can't wait to meet
him!

TorItUp: ☺ Can we chat later? I need to
finish this work.

SiennasHeart: Sure. See you tomorrow.
TGIF!

Yeah, she may be thanking God it's almost Friday but I'm not. That only leaves me a day to find Sebastian and convince him to come to the dance with me.

I return to my search results and click on page two. Oh, luck! Sebastian has a Buddiez page. I set up a page earlier in the summer but haven't been on it too much since. I log on to it and click on Sebastian's page. I click "Add Friend" and wait. And wait. And wait some more. I have this bad habit of thinking everyone is online at the exact time I am. He might not even be home. Maybe he's on the school football team and he's at practice right now. Or maybe he does volunteer work on Thursday afternoons. Or maybe he's suddenly getting hundreds of friend requests with his new fame so it takes him longer to go through and accept them.

Ugh. This isn't working. What am I going to do?

20

Isn't it strange how walking to homeroom can seem so much like walking to your own funeral? It's never felt like this before, of course, but now that there are only thirty-six short hours until the school dance where I am to make Sebastian magically appear in the flesh, it's feeling very funeral-y.

I make myself walk into the classroom, clutching my books to my chest so hard that my knuckles are turning white. Everyone is already here. I waited until the last possible second to come in, hoping that doing so would cut down on the chatting and unavoidable questions about Sebastian.

"Tori," Avery yells, waving.

Sea grins at me. "You're just in time. We're going over our outfits for tomorrow. I'm thinking of going with a concert tee, fitted black velvet vest, and my dark jeans."

"I'm wearing a pink minidress with my tall brown boots," Natalie announces. "My mom is trying to make me wear tights too, but I'm fighting it."

"I'm wearing jeans and a sparkly silver sweater that belts around the waist. It's new," Avery adds.

I nod and attempt a smile. "Your outfits sound great. I'm still not sure what I'm wearing." Seriously? Clothes have got to be about the last thing on my mind. More like the tenth thing *after* the last thing on my mind.

"Want me to come over and help you pick something out?" Sienna asks.

I'm temporarily speechless. She wants to help me pick out my outfit. *Now?* That's where this whole mess started. She was supposed to help me pick out my outfit for the first day of school, but she was MIA. She couldn't be bothered to call or e-mail or send a carrier pigeon. Nothing. Maybe if she'd just been there for me this summer I wouldn't be in this huge gigantic lying mess. Argh!

"Tori? You okay?" Sienna inquires. She's giving me a truly concerned look.

"Hmm?" I respond.

"You spaced out or something there. I asked if you wanted me to help you pick out an outfit for the dance tomorrow," Sea restates.

You know, I never ditched Sea like she did me this summer. And it isn't like the opportunity never arose.

I still remember it like it was yesterday. It was the fifth-grade field trip to Springfield. Claire Philips and Tess Aimes asked if I wanted to sit in the back of the bus with them. They said Sienna couldn't come though. It was a bad period in Sienna's life. Her mom had cut her bangs *way* too short, and waiting for them to grow out was excruciating for her. Kids teased her. But not me. *I'm* a true friend. I said, "Hey, you don't want my short-banged friend, then you don't want me." All right, maybe I'm remembering that a tad grander than it was. Actually, I think I shook my head no and slipped into the seat with Sienna in the middle of the bus. She gave me a grateful look and didn't say a word. But know what? She didn't need to. That's what best friends do.

"Tori," Sea calls out, shaking my shoulder.

"Oh, no. No thanks," I reply. I straighten up in my seat, facing the front of the room. Where the heck is the bell? There is entirely too much talking time for my liking.

"So, what did Sebastian say?" Sienna speaks to my back. "Is he coming to the dance?"

I plaster on a smile and turn around. "Yep. He can't wait to meet everyone," I say. I know, I know, but I've been lying so much these past two weeks, why stop now? I don't think there is much of a chance that I can make things any worse than they already are.

"Yay! It'll be fun. I bet him and Antonio get along great," she declares.

"I'm sure they will," I reply.

"My mom had the news on last night and that story about him and the fire came on. I told her how he was your boyfriend and she was like 'Wow, lucky girl,'" Avery tells us.

I smile. Lucky me!

Brinnnnnnng! There's that dang bell. I turn back around, facing the front of the room, and slump down in my seat.

I escape homeroom without any more incidents and head straight for science.

"Tori! We missed you yesterday," Daphne says as I slide into my seat.

"Yeah, I wasn't feeling so hot," I reply. I'm still not.

"Don't worry, you didn't miss a thing. The sub had us work silently on an old lab the entire hour. It was way boring," Bella says, tapping her pencil on her desk. "And she didn't even notice that you were gone."

I smile at Bella. "Thank you *so* much for that. I totally owe you."

"No prob," Bella replies.

The sub takes roll at an excruciatingly slow pace, butchering most of the students' names. I can't stop thinking about my e-mail. I haven't checked it since early this morning while I was getting ready for school. Maybe by some small miracle Sebastian got one of my e-mails and decided to take the chance that I wasn't a whackadoodle and responded. It could happen. I've heard lots of adults say miracles happen every day. I could get one. What else do I have to hold on to?

I raise my hand when roll call is over, and the sub calls on me. "Can I come up to your table and talk to you?" I ask.

She nods.

"Hi," I say when I reach her. "I'm Tori Barnes."

"Hi, Tori," the sub says.

"Did Mrs. Wittler leave you a note about me?" I ask.

She frowns and begins to leaf through the giant pile of papers before her. "Um, I don't think so," she finally says. "What's up?"

"I'm working on a special project. For the science fair. Mrs. Wittler lets me go to the library on Fridays to work on it," I state.

"Oh, of course. So, what do you need from me? A pass?" the sub replies without hesitation.

Wow. That was easy. Maybe I should ask her for more

stuff? No, I need to concentrate. I need to get to my e-mail. "Yeah, thanks."

The sub scribbles out a pass to the library, and I take it. I grab my stuff, wave to Daphne and Bella, and head out.

Minutes after I arrive in the library I'm seated at one of the computers and my e-mail is open. Nothing. Sigh.

I log on to Buddiez, still hanging on to a sliver of a thread of hope, and Oh. My. God! Oh my god, oh my god, oh my god. Sebastian Colander, the real, living, breathing Sebastian Colander, has accepted my friendship. I can't sit still. I want to dance. I want to channel all of my old Irish relatives and display my happiness in a jig. I jump out of my seat and clap my hands.

"Ahem."

I turn toward the checkout desk. Mrs. Cass is staring at me, one eyebrow raised, hands on hips in a no-nonsense pose. That's teacher for "settle down."

Message received loud and clear. "I'm sorry," I whisper and retake my seat.

My heart is racing though. This is *it*! Surely the universe is behind me 100 percent. This *is* going to somehow happen. Sebastian *will* come to the dance with me. Now that we're Buddiez friends I'll write him a note—a lovely note. Something warm and friendly, clever and charming, and not at all like a crazy weirdo Internet stalker. I'm sure I can get him to come to the dance tomorrow. All signs are pointing to yes, so how can he say no?

I click on Compose and stare at the giant empty box, waiting for the magical note to appear that will deliver Sebastian on my doorstep. Or the school steps if he'd prefer. Whatever.

Ugh, this is hard. I'm not sure what to say. If I were an eighth-grade boy and some girl wrote asking me to a dance, what would she have to say to get me to go? Aside from saying her name is Taylor Swift, of course. Even I can't pull off that lie. Maybe flattery? Maybe tell him it's my dying wish? No, that's mean. I can always tell him that I told the whole school he was my fake boyfriend and now that he's real I'd like to introduce him to everyone. No, then he really will think I'm a crazy person.

I'll just start typing and see what comes to me.

Dear Sebastian,
    Hello. I'd like to introduce myself. My name is Tori Barnes and I'm a seventh grader at Norton Junior High in Norton, IL. To be honest, I'm not very good at talking to boys. In fact, you're the first boy I've ever written to.

But I figured if I was going to take this huge
step and ask a boy to our school dance then I
wanted it to be an extra-special boy. Like you.
I guess I went and got right to the point of
why I'm writing. We have a dance in our
school gym here at Norton tomorrow and I
would be *so* honored if you would consider
going. With me. I heard about your heroics in
saving that family from the fire and I think you
are an amazing person. We can go to the
dance just as friends (Buddiez friends, LOL).
What do you say?
—Tori

There. I don't know if it will work, but I'm all out of
options. I've just got to hit . . .

Send.

And wait.

Thank goodness the last school bell has finally rung.
I've been waiting for it all day. I never did get online
again to see if Sebastian wrote me back, and the sus-
pense is seriously killing me. We're at T minus twenty-
eight hours until the dance.

I gather my books and stuff them into my backpack. I'm trying to hurry so I can be the first one on the bus and get one of the back seats. I really don't want to talk to anyone. I want to go home and get online.

I shuffle down the hallway, and Avery yells after me. "Bye, Tori! We'll see you tomorrow."

"And Sebastian too," Natalie adds.

I wave over my shoulder but don't turn around.

"Later, Tori," Daphne calls out as I pass her.

"Later," I reply.

The door is only a few feet ahead. I'm about to make it out of here.

"Tori! Wait," Sienna calls.

I freeze. Shoot. I was so close. I turn around. "Yes?"

"Do you want a ride home?" she asks.

"Oh, that's okay. The bus is fine. Really—"

"Don't be silly. My mom's car is right there." Sea points out the door to her mom. "C'mon."

Ugh. Just what I need. Ten minutes in the car with Sea talking nonstop about Antonio's visit, the dance with Antonio, the weekend with Antonio, blah blah blah all that boyfriend stuff. I'm going to lose it, I swear.

"Okay," I say anyway and follow her out to her car. At least it will get me home and in front of my e-mail faster than the bus would. I climb into the backseat.

"Hi, Tori," Sea's mom says.

"Hi, Mrs. Baker," I return.

Sienna climbs into the seat next to me. "Are you totally excited for tomorrow?"

"Oh. Yeah," I reply, trying to sound it.

"Me, too. Remember the back-to-school dance last year? When we went together?" Sienna asks.

"Of course." I smile. "Remember how we were too scared to dance with any boys the whole night? Not that any asked us."

"How could they? We spent most of the time standing by the soda machine." Sienna laughs. "We were kind of dorky last year."

I shrug. "Yeah. But I didn't mind."

Sienna looks thoughtful. "Well, we're sure not dorks this year."

"I guess not," I agree. We're both pretty quiet for the next few minutes, until we pull into my driveway.

"Want me to come in and help you pick out your outfit?" Sienna asks.

I shake my head. "It's okay. I'll see you tomorrow. Thanks for the ride!" I hop out of the car and run up to my house.

Once I've put the double lock on the front door, I practically run to my room and fling myself into my desk chair. I log on to my Buddiez, and *yes!* There *is* a reply from Sebastian Colander. I knew it. I'm literally shaking. Everything is going to work out.

I open the message and read.

Dear Tori,

    Hey. Thanks for the nice letter and invitation to your school's dance. Sounds like fun. Unfortunately, I can't make it. For one, I don't exactly know you. And my parents have this strict rule about me not meeting anyone off of the Internet. I'm sure you're a normal girl, but you never know when an old crazy bad guy is going to try and lure some kid somewhere, you know? For two, I'm only fourteen and I can't drive. And three, even if I could drive, my parents would never let me drive that far on my own. I'm real sorry. But hey, if you send me your address I can autograph my picture from the paper and drop it in the mail to you.

—Sebastian Colander

Huh. I wonder if his autograph can pop, lock, and drop it?

I'm so screwed.

21

I'm done. Finished. I've got nothing left—no more tricks in my bag. The end. I totally failed. But of course I failed. That's what happens when you lie, right? You don't win. You lose. Bill Clinton lied about hooking up with Monica Lewinsky. FAIL. Martha Stewart lied about illegally using a stock tip. FAIL. Tori Barnes lied about having a boyfriend named Sebastian Colander. FAIL.

Ahh! I can't face the world. I'm going to stay right here in my bed forever.

"Tori? You awake?" Mom calls from outside my bedroom door.

"No!" I yell.

"What? You sound muffled," she adds.

I pull the covers off my head and sit up in bed. "No!" I scream, and then flop back down.

Mom raps on my door. "Can I come in please?"

I stare at the ceiling. "If you must," I mumble.

Mom opens the door and walks over to my bed, her hand covering the mouthpiece of the phone.

Great. Just great. I am so not in the mood for any phone calls right now. I'm far too busy ruining my entire life to chat.

"Dad's on the phone, hon," she says, holding the phone out to me.

I shake my head. I'm not in the mood to talk to Dad either. I don't need him telling me again how he told me so.

Mom puts the phone back up to her ear. "Jason? Can Tori call you back later? She doesn't appear to be feeling well."

"Thanks," I mouth.

"You want me to tell her what?" Mom says. She gives me an odd look. "Okay, hold on, I'll tell her." She covers up the mouthpiece of the phone again. "Your dad wants me to tell you that he found that kid you're looking for and he wants to know if you want him to call him."

I'm suddenly feeling even worse than I was just a second ago. I didn't think it was possible. I wave my hands in front of my face. "No. Tell him *no way*. Under no circumstances is he to call him. Just forget I ever mentioned it."

Mom puts the phone back up to her ear. "Got all that?" she asks Dad. "Okay then. You too. Take care." She hangs up.

Mom takes a seat on my bed. "Tori? What was that about?"

"Nothing," I mutter gloomily.

"Sure doesn't sound like nothing," she continues.

"I don't want to talk about it," I reply.

She sits there for a moment. Probably waiting to see if I'm going to change my mind. When she finally talks she says, "Okay. You don't have to tell me. But if you want to, I'll listen. In the meantime, I have the entire day free, so I'm all yours. Want to go shopping and pick out something cute to wear to your dance tonight?"

Hmm. Well, I was kind of hoping I would catch a twenty-four-hour bug or something and not be able to go to the dance tonight. But maybe it's worth it to go to the mall. It's got to be easier to catch the flu in that people-packed place than in my reasonably clean room. And if I do still go to the dance, at least I'll look cute when everyone finds out I'm a big fraud. "Okay," I agree.

"Good." She nods. "Why don't you get dressed and meet me out front? We'll pick up breakfast at the mall." Mom gives me a cheery smile and leaves my room.

If she only knew what I've been up to these last two and a half weeks, I don't think she'd be smiling.

An hour later we're walking through our second store at the mall. I take a sip from my large frozen mocha. Mom doesn't let me drink coffee drinks unless I'm super upset and she's trying to cheer me up. She's talking about all kinds of stuff, really rambling on and on. She asks about my homework, if I'm going to dress up this year for Halloween, do I think I want to write for the school newspaper again, and so on. She's talking about everything under the sun *except* what's bothering me. She's so pointedly *not* talking about Dad's phone call or why I was upset this morning that it's starting to drive me nuts. It's such a total Mom maneuver intended to make me break down and spill.

I'm trying hard to resist her moves as we sit outside the small bakery in the food court, sharing a giant gooey cinnamon roll.

"Did you know your grandma used to make me and Aunt Kate homemade cinnamon rolls every single Sunday morning?" Mom says. "I would rest my chin on the kitchen counter and literally drool as I watched her stir the icing and then drip it onto the rolls. They were delicious." She pops a piece of the roll into her mouth.

"Okay! Fine! I'll tell you. Sheesh. Beat it out of me, why don't you?"

Mom smiles and wipes her mouth with a napkin. "I'm listening."

"Oh, Mom." My shoulders slump and my bottom lip quivers. I feel like I might cry.

Mom reaches out and rubs my hand. "It's okay, Tori. Take your time."

"I made a real mess of things, Mom. A really big mess," I start.

She nods, waiting for me to go on.

"Well, Sea stopped talking to me halfway through the summer. She didn't respond to my e-mails, nothing. Then she comes back looking all superstar, and the kids at school were falling all over her. She said she had this wonderful boyfriend who she met on vacation. His name's Antonio. I didn't believe her. I thought she was making him up. I got tired of listening to her go on and on, so I made up a fake boyfriend too. I told a lot of lies. I mean *a lot* of lies."

"Like what?" Mom asks.

"You name it, I said it. I said Sebastian Colander, that's my fake boyfriend, was calling me and IMing me. He sent me flowers, and he even gave me a Tiffany necklace." I stop, gauging her reaction to the necklace. But she doesn't say anything. "Well, there *is* a real Sebastian Colander. Who knew? The whole class saw him on the news this week. He lives in Chicago. He's a local hero. Everyone insisted that I bring him to the dance, and then Sea said *she* was bringing her boyfriend, Antonio.

Yeah, turns out her boyfriend is *real*. I was positive that she was lying the whole time, and I was just trying to one-up her. But now it's only me who's the liar. I don't know what to do, Mom," I say. I put my face in my hands.

Mom's quiet for a moment. "Tori," she finally begins, "I think you've already gathered that it's wrong to lie, correct?"

"Oh, I gather. I gather."

"Well, then you need to fix it. Tell Sienna the truth," she affirms.

"The truth? Now you sound just like Dad!" I argue.

"Your dad is right, Tori. And so am I. The only way to fix this is to tell Sienna everything. Tell her how you were feeling—that you were insecure."

I frown.

"She's your best friend, Tori. She's going to forgive you. But you've got to tell her the truth, and do it now before this thing gets any worse."

I fold my arms over my chest. "This sucks."

"I know, sweetie. But it's a good lesson. We all go through them. You're not the first kid to lie, you know," Mom states.

"Have you lied?"

Mom smiles. "Let's stay focused here, shall we?"

Darn.

"You need to go to the dance tonight and straighten

things out with Sienna," Mom says. "And believe me, tomorrow you'll feel twenty pounds lighter."

"Yeah, yeah," I mutter. "Dad already told me all that truth-sets-you-free stuff."

"You've got a smart dad, Tor."

22

Mom pulls up to the front doors of Norton Junior High and puts the car in park. I look down at my outfit. It *is* pretty cute. Mom bought me a new flowy skirt and T-shirt to wear tonight.

"C'mon, Tori," Mom urges. "You can do it. I know it."

"I'm glad one of us does," I return. I stare in through the glass doors. The lights are bright, and there are kids standing around smiling and talking in the entranceway.

Mom puts a hand on my shoulder. "Sweets, the sooner you get in there, the sooner it will be over with. Start by walking into school. Go on."

I grip the car door handle and look at the school entrance once more. I can't believe I'm really going to walk in there. Alone.

"I'll be back at nine to pick you up. Call if you need me to come sooner, okay?" Mom says.

Like if the crowd turns on me and they hang me from the rafters? I nod and step out of the car. A breeze hits me and I shiver.

I can do this, I can do this, I chant to myself.

I pass the kids lingering in the entranceway. Right now I'm trying to put one foot in front of the other.

I stand by the gym doors, ready to face the music. Hey, I made a funny. I would totally laugh if this wasn't the worst moment in my entire life. I open one of the heavy wood doors and walk in. The music is loud, and there is a gigantic mirrored disco ball hanging from some pipes near the gym ceiling. The DJ is wearing sunglasses and bopping around behind a table with a stereo on it. He looks like he's a high schooler. I scan the room looking for Sienna, but I don't see her yet. There are kids everywhere, and I totally expect them to be whispering to each other, "Where's Sebastian? Where's her boyfriend?" but no one is even looking at me.

Daphne and Bella stand underneath one of the basketball hoops, waving at me. They both look cute in short colorful cotton dresses—solid cranberry on Daphne and a burnt orange on Bella. I brace myself and march over to them. Before they can even say hi, I begin. "Listen," I say, talking fast, "there is no Sebastian

Colander, okay? Well, there *is* a Sebastian Colander. Just not one that I'm dating. I don't have a boyfriend. I made him up. I lied and I'm sorry." I take a deep breath. There. I got it out.

Daphne and Bella look at each other, confusion across their faces, and then look back at me.

"Tori," Daphne starts slowly, "what on earth are you talking about?"

"Sebastian," I repeat. "You know, my boyfriend, er, fake boyfriend."

The girls look at me blankly.

Oh my god. They *don't know.*

Okay, how does anyone not know? I thought everyone knew. Hadn't I mentioned Sebastian to Daphne and Bella? I'm sure I had. Maybe. Well, now that I replay the last weeks in my head, maybe I hadn't. Sheesh. Maybe it's my own big head now thinking that everyone is talking and obsessing about me and my life when really people are just doing their own thing, living their own lives, and I'm like a brief pop-up ad on their Buddiez home pages. Something you only take in for a moment and never really think about again.

"So, let me get this straight," I begin. "Not to sound like a loser or anything, but you guys like me? *Me,* me? Not me because I'm Sienna's best friend or because we have boyfriends but just because of me?"

The girls look at each other and laugh. "Uh, yeah," Daphne confirms.

"But, Daphne," I go on, "you made fun of my boots last year!"

"I did?" Daphne asks. "I'm so sorry. I was kind of mean last year. I was embarrassed because I wear a lot of knockoffs. That's all my mom buys me. I was probably trying to call you out to distract you from calling me out. But I don't care about that stuff anymore. I changed a lot this summer."

I nod. "A lot changed this summer," I agree. "Do you think we can maybe forget about all that stuff I just spewed out?"

"I already forgot," Bella replies.

"Me too. Short-term memory loss," Daphne adds, tapping her head.

"Thanks, guys." I smile.

"Oh, guess what?" Daphne asks. Her eyes are bright like she can't wait to spill some big news.

"What?" I ask.

"My mom has a friend on the school board, and I overheard them talking this morning about the whole Wittler thing. Turns out she's been drinking at schools for *years*," Daphne says dramatically.

"No way," I utter.

Bella nods. Daphne must have already told her.

"This is the third school she's been at in the last five years," Daphne continues, holding up three fingers for emphasis.

"It's the first time she got fired though," Bella adds.

"Yeah," Daphne picks up. "She got the last two schools to let her voluntarily resign so our school never knew when they hired her."

"Oh, man," I whisper, shaking my head.

"Principal Brown isn't letting her off so easy though. Wittler's in big trouble. She won't be partying at any more schools, that's for sure," Bella asserts.

"We're heroes," Daphne says proudly.

"I wouldn't go *that* far," I retort. I mean, I'm glad we got Wittler out of school, but I sure don't feel like a hero, especially not with what I still have to tell Sienna tonight. Speaking of Sea, where is she?

I turn around and look at the gym doors just in time to see her walk in with Antonio. He *is* gorgeous, of course. And they look gorgeous together. Sienna has her hair down and loose around her shoulders, and even though she did wear her jeans and vest over a T-shirt, she looks more like a rock star than a seventh grader. Antonio is about five inches taller than her with jet-black hair and dark eyes. He's wearing a tan polo shirt with worn-in jeans. He has an arm casually flung around her shoulder, and she looks like she belongs there.

"Will you guys excuse me?" I say to Daphne and Bella.

"Sure." Daphne nods. "We'll catch up with you later."

I walk toward Sienna and Antonio, wringing my hands the whole way. Though I've played this scene in my head a hundred times today, I can't be sure how it will come out of my mouth.

"Hey, Sea," I say when I reach them.

"Tori! Hey!" She looks almost giddy. "Tori, this is my boyfriend, Antonio. Antonio, this is my best friend in the whole world, Tori."

Antonio smiles. "Nice to meet you, Tori."

"Nice to meet you," I echo.

Sienna looks over my left shoulder and then around my right. "Where's Sebastian?" she asks.

"I sort of wanted to talk to you about that. Alone, if you don't mind. Sorry, Antonio," I add, looking at him.

Sienna nods, giving me a concerned look. "Want to go to the bathroom for privacy?"

"Yeah, that sounds like a good idea."

We walk quickly to the bathroom in the hallway, right outside our math classroom. My stomach churns

What I'm about to do is *huge*. What if
Sienna says, You know Tori, I'm so cool now I don't
need a liar for a best friend? What if she never speaks to
me again? I'll be so totally devastated.

Sienna goes into the bathroom first, checking underneath the stall doors to make sure we are alone. I
step up to one of the white ceramic sinks and crank on
the cold. I splash water on my face, not even caring
that I'm probably ruining the lip gloss and light mascara I put on only an hour earlier.

I rest my palms on the sink, close my eyes, and slowly
count to five to relax. When I turn around, Sienna is
leaning against the old rusty radiator giving me a concerned look.

"Okay, spill," she urges.

"It's just . . . This is so much harder than I thought
it was going to be," I mutter, more to myself than to
her. I drop my head and stare at the floor.

Sienna puts a hand on my shoulder. "What's wrong,
Tori? You look like you're going to cry. Wait," she says,
crossing her arms over her chest. "Did Sebastian break
up with you?"

I don't lift my head. Oooh. That isn't bad. It actually *might* work. I can pretend that Sebastian dumped
me right before the dance and . . .

No! No, I can't keep lying to Sienna like this. I have to come clean. I have to tell her the truth.

My eyes meet Sienna's. "Sea, I have to tell you something. And you may not be very happy with me after I tell you."

"Okay," she replies slowly.

"Um, this is hard. It's sort of like this: You know Sebastian Colander? He's not exactly my boyfriend."

Her eyes grow wide, but she doesn't say anything.

I start talking faster. "I made him up. There never was a Sebastian. Well, there *is* a Sebastian, but he didn't show up until much later and it was a total freakin' fluke. I don't know that kid that was on TV. He never was my boyfriend. I was hurt and mad because you went away for the whole summer, and at first you wrote me but then your e-mails got shorter and shorter, and then they stopped altogether. Like you couldn't even be bothered with me anymore. I was so lonely and bored. I missed you so much. And then you come back looking all"—I wave my hand at her—"different. I felt left behind, I guess."

I pick up a paper towel from the edge of the sink and twist it. Sea is still looking at me with no discernible expression on her face. "Then," I go on, "you said you had a boyfriend. And, don't be mad, but I thought you were lying. I could have *sworn* you made him up. So

I was trying to outdo you and have a better fake boy-friend. I don't know why, it was stupid. *I* was totally stupid."

I shift my weight from one foot to the other. "I guess what I'm trying to say is that I'm so, so sorry. I'm sorry for not believing you and I'm sorry for lying to you. And I really hope that you'll forgive me."

I look back down at the floor and wait for her reaction. I tighten my grip on the paper towel, ready for Sienna to totally yell at me and say my lies ruined our friendship or storm out of the bathroom. But she doesn't do either.

I take a chance and look up. I study her face, and there is the slightest hint of a smile.

"What?" I ask.

"Um, that's not Antonio out there waiting for me in the gym," Sienna says. "His name's Eddie. He's the son of one of my dad's co-workers. He looks like an Anto-nio, though, doesn't he? I had to give him my iPod to come to the dance with me tonight."

"What?" I repeat.

Sienna hops up on the counter between two of the sinks. "There is no Antonio. I made him up too."

I cover my mouth with my right hand. Oh my god! I can't believe this. "But why?" I finally say, through parted fingers.

Sienna crosses her legs at the ankle and swings them back and forth. "I don't know. I guess I decided that this was the year things were going to change for me. I figured if I came back from vacation seeming glamorous and important, everyone would think I really was. You have to admit it worked."

"Well, yeah. But couldn't you have filled me in on your plan?" I whine.

Sienna frowns. "I'm sorry. You're right. But in my defense, I really never planned on going on and on about Antonio, but when you started talking about Sebastian so much I got competitive. I wanted my boyfriend to be better than yours."

"He so wasn't," I say.

"Totally was," she counters, and we dissolve into giggles.

I abruptly stop laughing. "But wait," I say, putting a hand in the air. "What about the last part of the summer. Why did you stop talking to me, Sea?"

"Oh, Tor," she begins, twisting up her face. "Not talking to you was the worst part of the entire summer. But I knew I couldn't. If I'd kept talking to you, you would've known that Antonio was a fake and I wasn't doing anything fun. That all I did was collect seashells, eat ice cream cones, shop at lame little gift shops with my mom, and play chess with my dad. I needed you to believe my stories too or no one else would. I figured once you saw me—saw that I looked and acted different—you'd buy the boyfriend story too."

"Really?" I reply quietly. "Because my summer totally sucked without you, you know."

"I'm so, so sorry," Sea says. Her bottom lip quivers like she might cry, and I don't want her to do that.

"I'm sorry too," I say, and add quickly, "I mean, for everything."

Sienna jumps off of the counter, and I throw my arms around her neck.

"Oh, Sea, I can't tell you how relieved I am that you don't hate me. I really thought you were never going to talk to me again," I say.

"I could never hate you, Tori." She squeezes back and then pulls away. "But let's promise to never lie to each other again. Okay?"

"Deal."

Sienna glances at the bathroom door. "We better get back to Eddie, huh? He's probably wondering what happened to me."

"Yeah, let's go," I agree, and we head for the door. "Oh, wait." I grab her arm. "What do we tell people if they ask?"

Sienna thinks. "I've got it! Let's tell them that our boyfriends were getting in between us, and we decided our friendship was the most important thing."

I nod. "Yeah. Sounds perfect. *And* it's not a lie."

Sea smirks.

"One thing I learned from all this," I say, "is that I'm not ready for a boyfriend, real or fake."

"Me neither," Sea says as we head for the gym.

ACKNOWLEDGMENTS

It's amazing how many people go into making a book and how lost I'd be without them. First, I have to thank my amazing editor, Janine O'Malley, for sticking with me and offering lots of encouragement and wonderful insights. A heartfelt thank-you to the awesome FSG team for all that you've done for me. I'm thankful for my big wonderful family and my amazing friends—you guys are the best fan club ever! And a special thank-you to my four super cuties, Teegan, Maya, London, and Gavin, who think Mommy just drinks lots of coffee at the Starbucks at night even though she says she's writing books. Okay, I do both. Big hugs to my husband, Athens, for encouraging me to put off stuff that can be done later (yes, you evil dishes) and to get back to my writing. I am deeply grateful to my first readers, Deena Lipomi, Mandy Morgan, and Kristin Walker, who, besides being some of my favorite writers, are lightning-fast readers and so smart and right-on with

180

their notes. And for keeping me sane (and really, this isn't the easiest, we writers are weird), the 2009 Debs, the Author2Author girls (Deena, Emily, Kate, and Lisa), and all my Twitter, Facebook, and LiveJournal buds. And I couldn't possibly forget to leave off without one last giant thank-you to *my* seventh-grade fake boyfriend and the BFF who stole him away from me: SMOOCHES and thanks for the inspiration, guys!